DOVER · THRIFT · EDITIONS

Ghosts

HENRIK IBSEN

DOVER PUBLICATIONS, INC.
Mineola, New York

DOVER THRIFT EDITIONS

EDITOR OF THIS VOLUME: GLENN MOTT

Copyright

Published in Canada by General Publishing Company, Ltd., 30 Lesmill Road, Don Mills, Toronto, Ontario.

Theatrical Rights

Bibliographical Note

This Dover edition, first published in 1997, is an unabridged republication of the work translated by R. Farquharson Sharp, originally published in 1911 by J. M. Dent & Sons Ltd., New York. An introductory Note has been prepared specially for this edition.

Library of Congress Cataloging-in-Publication Data

Ibsen, Henrik, 1828–1906.
[Gengangere. English]
Ghosts / Henrik Ibsen.
p.   cm. — (Dover thrift editions)
ISBN 0-486-29852-3 (pbk.)
I. Title. II. Series.
PT8865.A333   1997
839.8'226—dc21   97-23684
                                                              CIP

Manufactured in the United States of America
Dover Publications, Inc., 31 East 2nd Street, Mineola, N.Y. 11501

Note

BEGINNING with *Pillars of Society* in 1877, the Norwegian poet and playwright Henrik Ibsen (1828–1906) wrote a group of realistic "problem plays" that constitute his most familiar and enduring work. The most notable of these are A *Doll's House* and *Ghosts*. In A *Doll's House*, he had drawn fire by having Nora slam the door forever on her husband Torvald. Ibsen was reproached for attacking the sanctity of marriage, lauded as a suffragist, and called by others an advocate of free love—labels that met Ibsen's indignation. The criticism of Nora was so intense, that Ibsen was persuaded at one point to write a new ending in which she returns for the sake of her children. But two years after A *Doll's House*, Ibsen had his real answer to the critics in *Ghosts'* Mrs. Alving. With her conventional respect for marriage, in spite of a dissolute husband, Mrs. Alving is the tragic antithesis of Nora.

Written in Italy in 1881, *Ghosts* was first produced in Chicago, in Norwegian, before making its way slowly across the stages of Europe. It dealt openly with venereal disease, incest, and euthanasia, which caught the ire of critics and earned the consternation of the public who thought *Ghosts* was primarily a play about Oswald's inherited illness, rather than the unhappy consequences of Mrs. Alving's conformity. At the time *Ghosts* was considered a naturalistic drama, and many people misread the conventions it attacked.

What makes the play a landmark is primarily a matter of form. *Ghosts* was written in an everyday prose, with a compact classical structure—at a time when classical unities had been largely abandoned. It recalls Greek tragedy in its austerity and inexorable unraveling, but unlike the *Agamemnon*, which is the result of breaking moral code, the tragedy in *Ghosts* is the result of Mrs. Alving's unwillingness to break it. In addition, Ibsen significantly altered the notion of dramatic action. The action in *Ghosts* is *a priori* to the rise of the curtain. What one gets is the intensification of a latent crisis as it is made public, revealing the inner lives and subterfuge of the characters. Ibsen's exposition calls for less external virtuosity from actors and requires a subtlety which, over time, has had a major influence on technique. These qualities have helped define modern drama, and established Ibsen as the foremost dramatist of his time.

Characters

MRS. ALVING, *a widow.*
OSWALD ALVING, *her son, an artist.*
MANDERS, *the Pastor of the parish.*
ENGSTRAND, *a carpenter.*
REGINA ENGSTRAND, *his daughter, in*
Mrs. Alving's service.

The action takes place at MRS. ALVING'S *house on one of the larger* *fjords of western Norway.*

Ghosts

ACT I

SCENE.—*A large room looking upon a garden. A door in the left-hand wall, and two in the right. In the middle of the room, a round table with chairs set about it, and books, magazines and newspapers upon it. In the foreground on the left, a window, by which is a small sofa with a work-table in front of it. At the back the room opens into a conservatory rather smaller than the room. From the right-hand side of this a door leads to the garden. Through the large panes of glass that form the outer wall of the conservatory, a gloomy fjord land-scape can be discerned, half obscured by steady rain.*

ENGSTRAND *is standing close up to the garden door. His left leg is slightly deformed, and he wears a boot with a clump of wood under the sole.* REGINA, *with an empty garden-syringe in her hand, is try-ing to prevent his coming in.*

Regina (below her breath). What is it you want? Stay where you are. The rain is dripping off you.

Engstrand. God's good rain, my girl.

Regina. The Devil's own rain, that's what it is!

Engstrand. Lord, how you talk, Regina. *(Takes a few limping steps forward.)* What I wanted to tell you was this ———

Regina. Don't clump about like that, stupid! The young master is lying asleep upstairs.

Engstrand. Asleep still? In the middle of the day?

Regina. Well, it's no business of yours.

Engstrand. I was out on the spree last night———

Regina. I don't doubt it.

Engstrand. Yes, we are poor weak mortals, my girl———

Regina. We are indeed.

Engstrand. —and the temptations of the world are manifold, you know—but, for all that, here I was at my work at half-past five this morning.

Regina. Yes, yes, but make yourself scarce now. I am not going to stand here as if I had a *rendez-vous* with you.

Engstrand. As if you had a what?

Regina. I am not going to have any one find you here; so now you know, and you can go.

1

Engstrand (coming a few steps nearer).   Not a bit of it! Not before we have had a little chat. This afternoon I shall have finished my job down at the school house, and I shall be off home to town by to-night's boat.

Regina (mutters).   Pleasant journey to you!

Engstrand.   Thanks, my girl! To-morrow is the opening of the Orphanage, and I expect there will be a fine kick-up here and plenty of good strong drink, don't you know. And no one shall say of Jacob Engstrand that he can't hold off when temptation comes in his way.

Regina.   Oho!

Engstrand.   Yes, because there will be a lot of fine folk here to-morrow. Parson Manders is expected from town, too.

Regina.   What is more, he's coming to-day.

Engstrand.   There you are! And I'm going to be precious careful he doesn't have anything to say against me, do you see?

Regina.   Oh, that's your game, is it?

Engstrand.   What do you mean?

Regina (with a significant look at him).   What is it you want to humbug Mr. Manders out of, this time?

Engstrand.   Sh! Sh! Are you crazy? Do you suppose *I* would want to humbug Mr. Manders? No, no—Mr. Manders has always been too kind a friend for me to do that. But what I wanted to talk to you about, was my going back home to-night.

Regina.   The sooner you go, the better I shall be pleased.

Engstrand.   Yes, only I want to take you with me, Regina.

Regina (open-mouthed).   You want to take me———? What did you say?

Engstrand.   I want to take you home with me, I said.

Regina (contemptuously).   You will never get me home with you.

Engstrand.   Ah, we shall see about that.

Regina.   Yes, you can be quite certain we *shall* see about that. I, who have been brought up by a lady like Mrs. Alving?—I, who have been treated almost as if I were her own child?—do you suppose I am going home with *you?*—to such a house as yours? Not likely!

Engstrand.   What the devil do you mean? Are you setting yourself up against your father, you hussy?

Regina (mutters, without looking at him).   You have often told me I was none of yours.

Engstrand.   Bah!—why do you want to pay any attention to that?

Regina.   Haven't you many and many a time abused me and called me a———? For shame!

Engstrand. I'll swear I never used such an ugly word.

Regina. Oh, it doesn't matter what word you used.

Engstrand. Besides, that was only when I was a bit fuddled—hm! Temptations are manifold in this world, Regina.

Regina. Ugh!

Engstrand. And it was when your mother was in a nasty temper. I had to find some way of getting my knife into her, my girl. She was always so precious genteel. (*Mimicking her.*) "Let go, Jacob! Let me be! Please to remember that I was three years with the Alvings at Rosenvold, and they were people who went to Court!" (*Laughs.*) Bless my soul, she never could forget that Captain Alving got a Court appointment while she was in service here.

Regina. Poor mother—you worried her into her grave pretty soon.

Engstrand (shrugging his shoulders). Of course, of course; I have got to take the blame for everything.

Regina (beneath her breath, as she turns away). Ugh—that leg, too!

Engstrand. What are you saying, my girl?

Regina. Pied de mounton.

Engstrand. Is that English?

Regina. Yes.

Engstrand. You have had a good education out here, and no mistake; and it may stand you in good stead now, Regina.

Regina (after a short silence). And what was it you wanted me to come to town for?

Engstrand. Need you ask why a father wants his only child? Ain't I a poor lonely widower?

Regina. Oh, don't come to me with that tale. Why do you want me to go?

Engstrand. Well, I must tell you I am thinking of taking up a new line now.

Regina (whistles). You have tried that so often—but it has always proved a fool's errand.

Engstrand. Ah, but this time you will just see, Regina! Strike me dead if ———

Regina (stamping her feet). Stop swearing!

Engstrand. Sh! Sh!—you're quite right, my girl, quite right! What I wanted to say was only this, that I have put by a tidy penny out of what I have made by working at this new Orphanage up here.

Regina. Have you? All the better for you.

Engstrand. What is there for a man to spend his money on, out here in the country?

Regina. Well, what then?

Engstrand. Well, you see, I thought of putting the money into something that would pay. I thought of some kind of an eating-house for seafaring folk———

Regina. Heavens!

Engstrand. Oh, a high-class eating-house, of course,—not a pigsty for common sailors. Damn it, no; it would be a place ships' captains and first mates would come to; really good sort of people, you know.

Regina. And what should I———?

Engstrand. You would help there. But only to make a show, you know. You wouldn't find it hard work, I can promise you, my girl. You should do exactly as you liked.

Regina. Oh, yes, quite so!

Engstrand. But we must have some women in the house; that is as clear as daylight. Because in the evening we must make the place a little attractive—some singing and dancing, and that sort of thing. Remember they are seafolk—wayfarers on the waters of life! (*Coming nearer to her.*) Now don't be a fool and stand in your own way, Regina. What good are you going to do here? Will this education, that your mistress has paid for, be of any use? You are to look after the children in the new Home, I hear. Is that the sort of work for you? Are you so frightfully anxious to go and wear out your health and strength for the sake of these dirty brats?

Regina. No, if things were to go as I want them to, then———. Well, it may happen; who knows? It may happen!

Engstrand. What may happen?

Regina. Never you mind. Is it much that you have put by, up here?

Engstrand. Taking it all round, I should say about forty or fifty pounds.

Regina. That's not so bad.

Engstrand. It's enough to make a start with, my girl.

Regina. Don't you mean to give me any of the money?

Engstrand. No, I'm hanged if I do.

Regina. Don't you mean to send me as much as a dress-length of stuff, just for once?

Engstrand. Come and live in the town with me and you shall have plenty of dresses.

Regina. Pooh!—I can get that much for myself, if I have a mind to.

Engstrand. But it's far better to have a father's guiding hand,

Regina. Just now I can get a nice house in Little Harbour Street. They don't want much money down for it—and we could make it like a sort of seamen's home, don't you know.

Regina. But I have no intention of living with you! I have nothing whatever to do with you. So now, be off!

Engstrand. You wouldn't be living with me long, my girl. No such luck—not if you knew how to play your cards. Such a fine wench as you have grown this last year or two—

Regina. Well———?

Engstrand. It wouldn't be very long before some first mate came along—or perhaps a captain.

Regina. I don't mean to marry a man of that sort. Sailors have no *savoir-vivre*.

Engstrand. What haven't they got?

Regina. I know what sailors are, I tell you. They aren't the sort of people to marry.

Engstrand. Well, don't bother about marrying them. You can make it pay just as well. *(More confidentially.)* That fellow—the English-man—the one with the yacht—he gave seventy pounds, he did; and she wasn't a bit prettier than you.

Regina (advancing towards him). Get out!

Engstrand (stepping back). Here! here!—you're not going to hit me, I suppose?

Regina. Yes! If you talk like that of mother, I will hit you. Get out, I tell you! *(Pushes him up to the garden door.)* And don't bang the doors. Young Mr. Alving———

Engstrand. Is asleep—I know. It's funny how anxious you are about young Mr. Alving. *(In a lower tone.)* Oho! is it possible that it is *he* that———?

Regina. Get out, and be quick about it! Your wits are wandering, my good man. No, don't go that way; Mr. Manders is just coming along. Be off down the kitchen stairs.

Engstrand (moving towards the right). Yes, yes—all right. But have a bit of a chat with him that's coming along. He's the chap to tell you what a child owes to its father. For I am your father, anyway, you know. I can prove it by the Register.

[*He goes out through the farther door which* REGINA *has opened. She shuts it after him, looks hastily at herself in the mirror, fans herself with her handkerchief and sets her collar straight; then busies herself with the flowers.* MANDERS *enters the conservatory through the garden door. He wears an overcoat, carries an umbrella and has a small travelling-bag slung over his shoulder on a strap.*]

Manders. Good morning, Miss Engstrand.

Regina (turning round with a look of pleased surprise). Oh, Mr. Manders, good morning. The boat is in, then?

Manders. Just in. *(Comes into the room.)* It is most tiresome, this rain every day.

Regina (following him in). It's a splendid rain for the farmers, Mr. Manders.

Manders. Yes, you are quite right. We town-folk think so little about that.

[*Begins to take off his overcoat.*]

Regina. Oh, let me help you. That's it. Why, how wet it is! I will hang it up in the hall. Give me your umbrella, too; I will leave it open, so that it will dry.

[*She goes out with the things by the farther door on the right.* MANDERS *lays his bag and his hat down on a chair.* REGINA *re-enters.*]

Manders. Ah, it's very pleasant to get indoors. Well, is everything going on well here?

Regina. Yes, thanks.

Manders. Properly busy, though, I expect, getting ready for to-morrow?

Regina. Oh, yes, there is plenty to do.

Manders. And Mrs. Alving is at home, I hope?

Regina. Yes, she is. She has just gone upstairs to take the young master his chocolate.

Manders. Tell me—I heard down at the pier that Oswald had come back.

Regina. Yes, he came the day before yesterday. We didn't expect him till to-day.

Manders. Strong and well, I hope?

Regina. Yes, thank you, well enough. But dreadfully tired after his journey. He came straight from Paris without a stop—I mean, he came all the way without breaking his journey. I fancy he is having a sleep now, so we must talk a little bit more quietly, if you don't mind.

Manders. All right, we will be very quiet.

Regina (while she moves an armchair up to the table). Please sit down, Mr. Manders, and make yourself at home. *(He sits down; she puts a footstool under his feet.)* There! Is that comfortable?

Manders. Thank you, thank you. That is most comfortable. *(Looks at her.)* I'll tell you what, Miss Engstrand, I certainly think you have grown since I saw you last.

Regina. Do you think so? Mrs. Alving says, too, that I have developed.

Manders. Developed? Well, perhaps a little—just suitably.

[*A short pause.*]

Regina. Shall I tell Mrs. Alving you are here?

Manders. Thanks, there is no hurry, my dear child.—Now tell me, Regina my dear, how has your father been getting on here?

Regina. Thank you, Mr. Manders, he is getting on pretty well.

Manders. He came to see me, the last time he was in town.

Regina. Did he? He is always so glad when he can have a chat with you.

Manders. And I suppose you have seen him pretty regularly every day?

Regina. I? Oh, yes, I do—whenever I have time, that is to say.

Manders. Your father has not a very strong character, Miss Engstrand. He sadly needs a guiding hand.

Regina. Yes, I can quite believe that.

Manders. He needs someone with him that he can cling to, someone whose judgment he can rely on. He acknowledged that freely himself, the last time he came up to see me.

Regina. Yes, he has said something of the same sort to me. But I don't know whether Mrs. Alving could do without me—most of all just now, when we have the new Orphanage to see about. And I should be dreadfully unwilling to leave Mrs. Alving, too; she has always been so good to me.

Manders. But a daughter's duty, my good child———. Naturally we should have to get your mistress's consent first.

Regina. Still I don't know whether it would be quite the thing, at my age, to keep house for a single man.

Manders. What!! My dear Miss Engstrand, it is your own father we are speaking of!

Regina. Yes, I dare say, but still———. Now, if it were in a good house and with a real gentleman———

Manders. But, my dear Regina———

Regina. ———one whom I could feel an affection for, and really feel in the position of a daughter to———

Manders. Come, come—my dear good child———

Regina. I should like very much to live in town. Out here it is terribly lonely; and you know yourself, Mr. Manders, what it is to be alone in the world. And, though I say it, I really am both capable and willing. Don't you know any place that would be suitable for me, Mr. Manders?

Manders. I? No, indeed I don't.

Regina. But, dear Mr. Manders—at any rate don't forget me, in case——

Manders (getting up). No, I won't forget you, Miss Engstrand.

Regina. Because, if I——

Manders. Perhaps you will be so kind as to let Mrs. Alving know I am here?

Regina. I will fetch her at once, Mr. Manders.

[*Goes out to the left.* MANDERS *walks up and down the room once or twice, stands for a moment at the farther end of the room with his hands behind his back and looks out into the garden. Then he comes back to the table, takes up a book and looks at the title page, gives a start and looks at some of the others.*]

Manders. Hm!—Really!

[MRS. ALVING *comes in by the door on the left. She is followed by* REGINA, *who goes out again at once through the nearer door on the right.*]

Mrs. Alving (holding out her hand). I am very glad to see you, Mr. Manders.

Manders. How do you do, Mrs. Alving. Here I am, as I promised.

Mrs. Alving. Always punctual!

Manders. Indeed, I was hard put to it to get away. What with vestry meetings and committees——

Mrs. Alving. It was all the kinder of you to come in such good time; we can settle our business before dinner. But where is your luggage?

Manders (quickly). My things are down at the village shop. I am going to sleep there to-night.

Mrs. Alving (repressing a smile). Can't I really persuade you to stay the night here this time?

Manders. No, no; many thanks all the same; I will put up there, as usual. It is so handy for getting on board the boat again.

Mrs. Alving. Of course you shall do as you please. But it seems to me quite another thing, now we are two old people——

Manders. Ha! ha! You will have your joke! And it's natural you should be in high spirits to-day—first of all there is the great event to-morrow, and also you have got Oswald home.

Mrs. Alving. Yes, am I not a lucky woman! It is more than two years since he was home last, and he has promised to stay the whole winter with me.

Manders. Has he, really? That is very nice and filial of him; because there must be many more attractions in his life in Rome or in Paris, I should think.

Mrs. Alving. Yes, but he has his mother here, you see. Bless the dear boy, he has got a corner in his heart for his mother still.

Manders. Oh, it would be very sad if absence and preoccupation with such a thing as Art were to dull the natural affections.

Mrs. Alving. It would, indeed. But there is no fear of that with him, I am glad to say. I am quite curious to see if you recognise him again. He will be down directly; he is just lying down for a little on the sofa upstairs. But do sit down, my dear friend.

Manders. Thank you. You are sure I am not disturbing you?

Mrs. Alving. Of course not.

[*She sits down at the table.*]

Manders. Good. Then I will show you————. (*He goes to the chair where his bag is lying and takes a packet of papers from it; then sits down at the opposite side of the table and looks for a clear space to put the papers down.*) Now first of all, here is—(*breaks off*). Tell me, Mrs. Alving, what are these books doing here?

Mrs. Alving. These books? I am reading them.

Manders. Do you read this sort of thing?

Mrs. Alving. Certainly I do.

Manders. Do you feel any the better or the happier for reading books of this kind?

Mrs. Alving. I think it makes me, as it were, more self-reliant.

Manders. That is remarkable. But why?

Mrs. Alving. Well, they give me an explanation or a confirmation of lots of different ideas that have come into my own mind. But what surprises me, Mr. Manders, is that, properly speaking, there is nothing at all new in these books. There is nothing more in them than what most people think and believe. The only thing is, that most people either take no account of it or won't admit it to themselves.

Manders. But, good heavens, do you seriously think that most people————?

Mrs. Alving. Yes, indeed, I do.

Manders. But not here in the country at any rate? Not here amongst people like ourselves?

Mrs. Alving. Yes, amongst people like ourselves too.

Manders. Well, really, I must say————!

Mrs. Alving. But what is the particular objection that you have to these books?

Manders. What objection? You surely don't suppose that I take any particular interest in such productions?

Mrs. Alving. In fact, you don't know anything about what you are denouncing?

Manders. I have read quite enough about these books to disapprove of them.

Mrs. Alving. Yes, but your own opinion————

Manders. My dear Mrs. Alving, there are many occasions in life when one has to rely on the opinion of others. That is the way in this world, and it is quite right that it should be so. What would become of society, otherwise?

Mrs. Alving. Well, you may be right.

Manders. Apart from that, naturally I don't deny that literature of this kind may have a considerable attraction. And I cannot blame you, either, for wishing to make yourself acquainted with the intellectual tendencies which I am told are at work in the wider world in which you have allowed your son to wander for so long. But————

Mrs. Alving. But————?

Manders (lowering his voice). But one doesn't talk about it, Mrs. Alving. One certainly is not called upon to account to everyone for what one reads or thinks in the privacy of one's own room.

Mrs. Alving. Certainly not. I quite agree with you.

Manders. Just think of the consideration you owe to this Orphanage, which you decided to build at a time when your thoughts on such subjects were very different from what they are now—as far as I am able to judge.

Mrs. Alving. Yes, I freely admit that. But it was about the Orphanage————

Manders. It was about the Orphanage we were going to talk; quite so. Well—walk warily, dear Mrs. Alving! And now let us turn to the business in hand. *(Opens an envelope and takes out some papers.)* You see these?

Mrs. Alving. The deeds?

Manders. Yes, the whole lot—and everything in order. I can tell you it has been no easy matter to get them in time. I had positively to put pressure on the authorities; they are almost painfully conscientious when it is a question of settling property. But here they are at last. *(Turns over the papers.)* Here is the deed of conveyance of that part of the Rosenvold estate known as the Solvik property, together with the buildings newly erected thereon—the school, the masters' houses and the chapel. And here is the legal sanction for the statutes of the institution. Here, you see—*(reads)* "Statutes for the Captain Alving Orphanage."

Mrs. Alving (after a long look at the papers).   That seems all in order.

Manders.   I thought "Captain" was the better title to use, rather than your husband's Court title of "Chamberlain." "Captain" seems less ostentatious.

Mrs. Alving.   Yes, yes; just as you think best.

Manders.   And here is the certificate for the investment of the capital in the bank, the interest being earmarked for the current expenses of the Orphanage.

Mrs. Alving.   Many thanks; but I think it will be most convenient if you will kindly take charge of them.

Manders.   With pleasure. I think it will be best to leave the money in the bank for the present. The interest is not very high, it is true; four per cent at six months' call. Later on, if we can find some good mortgage—of course it must be a first mortgage and on unexceptionable security—we can consider the matter further.

Mrs. Alving.   Yes, yes, my dear Mr. Manders, you know best about all that.

Manders.   I will keep my eye on it, anyway. But there is one thing in connection with it that I have often meant to ask you about.

Mrs. Alving.   What is that?

Manders.   Shall we insure the buildings, or not?

Mrs. Alving.   Of course we must insure them.

Manders.   Ah, but wait a moment, dear lady. Let us look into the matter a little more closely.

Mrs. Alving.   Everything of mine is insured—the house and its contents, my livestock—everything.

Manders.   Naturally. They are your own property. I do exactly the same, of course. But this, you see, is quite a different case. The Orphanage is, so to speak, dedicated to higher uses.

Mrs. Alving.   Certainly, but——

Manders.   As far as I am personally concerned, I can conscientiously say that I don't see the smallest objection to our insuring ourselves against all risks.

Mrs. Alving.   That is exactly what I think.

Manders. But what about the opinion of the people hereabouts?

Mrs. Alving. Their opinion———?

Manders. Is there any considerable body of opinion here—opinion of some account, I mean—that might take exception to it?

Mrs. Alving. What, exactly, do you mean by opinion of some account?

Manders. Well, I was thinking particularly of persons of such independent and influential position that one could hardly refuse to attach weight to their opinion.

Mrs. Alving. There are a certain number of such people here who might perhaps take exception to it if we———

Manders. That's just it, you see. In town there are lots of them. All my fellow-clergymen's congregations, for instance! It would be so extremely easy for them to interpret it as meaning that neither you nor I had a proper reliance on Divine protection.

Mrs. Alving. But as far as you are concerned, my dear friend, you have at all events the consciousness that———

Manders. Yes, I know, I know; my own mind is quite easy about it, it is true. But we should not be able to prevent a wrong and injurious interpretation of our action. And that sort of thing, moreover, might very easily end in exercising a hampering influence on the work of the Orphanage.

Mrs. Alving. Oh, well, if that is likely to be the effect of it———

Manders. Nor can I entirely overlook the difficult—indeed, I may say, painful—position I might possibly be placed in. In the best circles in town the matter of this Orphanage is attracting a great deal of attention. Indeed the Orphanage is to some extent built for the benefit of the town too, and it is to be hoped that it may result in the lowering of our poor-rate by a considerable amount. But as I have been your adviser in the matter and have taken charge of the business side of it, I should be afraid that it would be I that spiteful persons would attack first of all———

Mrs. Alving. Yes, you ought not to expose yourself to that.

Manders. Not to mention the attacks that would undoubtedly be made upon me in certain newspapers and reviews———

Mrs. Alving. Say no more about it, dear Mr. Manders; that quite decides it.

Manders. Then you don't wish it to be insured?

Mrs. Alving. No, we will give up the idea.

Manders (leaning back in his chair). But suppose, now, that some accident happened?—one can never tell—would you be prepared to make good the damage?

Mrs. Alving. No; I tell you quite plainly I would not do so under any circumstances.

Manders. Still, you know, Mrs. Alving—after all, it is a serious responsibility that we are taking upon ourselves.

Mrs. Alving. But do you think we can do otherwise?

Manders. No, that's just it. We really can't do otherwise. We ought not to expose ourselves to a mistaken judgment; and we have no right to do anything that will scandalise the community.

Mrs. Alving. You ought not to, as a clergyman, at any rate.

Manders. And, what is more, I certainly think that we may count upon our enterprise being attended by good fortune—indeed, that it will be under a special protection.

Mrs. Alving. Let us hope so, Mr. Manders.

Manders. Then we will leave it alone?

Mrs. Alving. Certainly.

Manders. Very good. As you wish. (*Makes a note.*) No insurance, then.

Mrs. Alving. It's a funny thing that you should just have happened to speak about that to-day———

Manders. I have often meant to ask you about it———

Mrs. Alving. ———because yesterday we very nearly had a fire up there.

Manders. Do you mean it!

Mrs. Alving. Oh, as a matter of fact it was nothing of any consequence. Some shavings in the carpenter's shop caught fire.

Manders. Where Engstrand works?

Mrs. Alving. Yes. They say he is often so careless with matches.

Manders. He has so many things on his mind, poor fellow—so many anxieties. Heaven be thanked, I am told he is really making an effort to live a blameless life.

Mrs. Alving. Really? Who told you so?

Manders. He assured me himself that it is so. He's a good workman, too.

Mrs. Alving. Oh, yes, when he is sober.

Manders. Ah, that sad weakness of his! But the pain in his poor leg often drives him to it, he tells me. The last time he was in town, I was really quite touched by him. He came to my house and thanked me so gratefully for getting him work here, where he could have the chance of being with Regina.

Mrs. Alving.   He doesn't see very much of her.

Manders.   But he assured me that he saw her every day.

Mrs. Alving.   Oh well, perhaps he does.

Manders.   He feels so strongly that he needs someone who can keep a hold on him when temptations assail him. That is the most winning thing about Jacob Engstrand; he comes to one like a helpless child and accuses himself and confesses his frailty. The last time he came and had a talk with me————. Suppose now, Mrs. Alving, that it were really a necessity of his existence to have Regina at home with him again————

Mrs. Alving (standing up suddenly).   Regina!

Manders.   ————you ought not to set yourself against him.

Mrs. Alving.   Indeed, I set myself very definitely against that. And, besides, you know Regina is to have a post in the Orphanage.

Manders.   But consider, after all he is her father————

Mrs. Alving.   I know best what sort of a father he has been to her. No, she shall never go to him with my consent.

Manders (getting up).   My dear lady, don't judge so hastily. It is very sad how you misjudge poor Engstrand. One would really think you were afraid————

Mrs. Alving (more calmly).   That is not the question. I have taken Regina into my charge, and in my charge she remains. *(Listens.)* Hush, dear Mr. Manders, don't say any more about it. *(Her face brightens with pleasure.)* Listen! Oswald is coming downstairs. We will only think about him now.

[OSWALD ALVING, *in a light overcoat, hat in hand and smoking a big meerschaum pipe, comes in by the door on the left.*]

Oswald (standing in the doorway).   Oh, I beg your pardon, I thought you were in the office. *(Comes in.)* Good morning, Mr. Manders.

Manders (staring at him).   Well! It's most extraordinary————

Mrs. Alving.   Yes, what do you think of him, Mr. Manders?

Manders.   I—I—no, can it possibly be————?

Oswald.   Yes, it really is the prodigal son, Mr. Manders.

Manders.   Oh, my dear young friend————

Oswald.   Well, the son come home, then.

Mrs. Alving.   Oswald is thinking of the time when you were so opposed to the idea of his being a painter.

Manders.   We are only fallible, and many steps seem to us hazardous at first, that afterwards—*(grasps his hand)*. Welcome, welcome! Really, my dear Oswald—may I still call you Oswald?

Oswald. What else would you think of calling me?

Manders. Thank you. What I mean, my dear Oswald, is that you must not imagine that I have any unqualified disapproval of the artist's life. I admit that there are many who, even in that career, can keep the inner man free from harm.

Oswald. Let us hope so.

Mrs. Alving (beaming with pleasure). I know one who has kept both the inner and the outer man free from harm. Just take a look at him, Mr. Manders.

Oswald (walks across the room). Yes, yes, mother dear, of course.

Manders. Undoubtedly—no one can deny it. And I hear you have begun to make a name for yourself. I have often seen mention of you in the papers—and extremely favourable mention, too. Although, I must admit, latterly I have not seen your name so often.

Oswald (going towards the conservatory). I haven't done so much painting just lately.

Mrs. Alving. An artist must take a rest sometimes, like other people.

Manders. Of course, of course. At those times the artist is preparing and strengthening himself for a greater effort.

Oswald. Yes. Mother, will dinner soon be ready?

Mrs. Alving. In half an hour. He has a fine appetite, thank goodness.

Manders. And a liking for tobacco too.

Oswald. I found father's pipe in the room upstairs, and———

Manders. Ah, that is what it was!

Mrs. Alving. What?

Manders. When Oswald came in at that door with the pipe in his mouth, I thought for the moment it was his father in the flesh.

Oswald. Really?

Mrs. Alving. How can you say so! Oswald takes after me.

Manders. Yes, but there is an expression about the corners of his mouth—something about the lips—that reminds me so exactly of Mr. Alving—especially when he smokes.

Mrs. Alving. I don't think so at all. To my mind, Oswald has much more of a clergyman's mouth.

Manders. Well, yes—a good many of my colleagues in the church have a similar expression.

Mrs. Alving. But put your pipe down, my dear boy. I don't allow any smoking in here.

Oswald (puts down his pipe). All right, I only wanted to try it, because I smoked it once when I was a child.

Mrs. Alving. You?

Oswald. Yes; it was when I was quite a little chap. And I can remember going upstairs to father's room one evening when he was in very good spirits.

Mrs. Alving. Oh, you can't remember anything about those days.

Oswald. Yes, I remember plainly that he took me on his knee and let me smoke his pipe. "Smoke, my boy," he said, "have a good smoke, boy!" And I smoked as hard as I could, until I felt I was turning quite pale and the perspiration was standing in great drops on my forehead. Then he laughed—such a hearty laugh——

Manders. It was an extremely odd thing to do.

Mrs. Alving. Dear Mr. Manders, Oswald only dreamt it.

Oswald. No indeed, mother, it was no dream. Because—don't you remember—you came into the room and carried me off to the nursery, where I was sick, and I saw that you were crying. Did father often play such tricks?

Manders. In his young days he was full of fun——

Oswald. And, for all that, he did so much with his life—so much that was good and useful, I mean—short as his life was.

Manders. Yes, my dear Oswald Alving, you have inherited the name of a man who undoubtedly was both energetic and worthy. Let us hope it will be a spur to your energies——

Oswald. It ought to be, certainly.

Manders. In any case it was nice of you to come home for the day that is to honour his memory.

Oswald. I could do no less for my father.

Mrs. Alving. And to let me keep him so long here—that's the nicest part of what he has done.

Manders. Yes, I hear you are going to spend the winter at home.

Oswald. I am here for an indefinite time, Mr. Manders.—Oh, it's good to be at home again!

Mrs. Alving (beaming). Yes, isn't it?

Manders (looking sympathetically at him). You went out into the world very young, my dear Oswald.

Oswald. I did. Sometimes I wonder if I wasn't too young.

Mrs. Alving. Not a bit of it. It is the best thing for an active boy, and especially for an only child. It's a pity when they are kept at home with their parents and get spoilt.

Manders. That is a very debatable question, Mrs. Alving. A child's own home is, and always must be, his proper place.

Oswald. There I agree entirely with Mr. Manders.

Manders. Take the case of your own son. Oh yes, we can talk about it before him. What has the result been in his case? He is six or seven and twenty, and has never yet had the opportunity of learning what a well-regulated home means.

Oswald. Excuse me, Mr. Manders, you are quite wrong there.

Manders. Indeed? I imagined that your life abroad had practically been spent entirely in artistic circles.

Oswald. So it has.

Manders. And chiefly amongst the younger artists.

Oswald. Certainly.

Manders. But I imagined that those gentry, as a rule, had not the means necessary for family life and the support of a home.

Oswald. There are a considerable number of them who have not the means to marry, Mr. Manders.

Manders. That is exactly my point.

Oswald. But they can have a home of their own, all the same; a good many of them have. And they are very well-regulated and very comfortable homes, too.

[MRS. ALVING, *who has listened to him attentively, nods assent, but says nothing.*]

Manders. Oh, but I am not talking of bachelor establishments. By a home I mean family life—the life a man lives with his wife and children.

Oswald. Exactly, or with his children and his children's mother.

Manders (starts and clasps his hands). Good heavens!

Oswald. What is the matter?

Manders. Lives with—with—his children's mother!

Oswald. Well, would you rather he should repudiate his children's mother?

Manders. Then what you are speaking of are those unprincipled conditions known as irregular unions!

Oswald. I have never noticed anything particularly unprincipled about these people's lives.

Manders. But do you mean to say that it is possible for a man of any sort of bringing up, and a young woman, to reconcile themselves to such a way of living—and to make no secret of it, either?

Oswald. What else are they to do? A poor artist, and a poor girl— it costs a good deal to get married. What else are they to do?

Manders. What are they to do? Well, Mr. Alving, I will tell you what they ought to do. They ought to keep away from each other from the very beginning—that is what they ought to do!

Oswald.   That advice wouldn't have much effect upon hot-blooded young folk who are in love.

Mrs. Alving.   No, indeed it wouldn't.

Manders (persistently).   And to think that the authorities tolerate such things! That they are allowed to go on, openly! *(Turns to* Mrs. Alving.*)* Had I so little reason, then, to be sadly concerned about your son? In circles where open immorality is rampant—where, one may say, it is honoured————

Oswald.   Let me tell you this, Mr. Manders. I have been a constant Sunday guest at one or two of these "irregular" households————

Manders.   On Sunday, too!

Oswald.   Yes, that is the day of leisure. But never have I heard one objectionable word there, still less have I ever seen anything that could be called immoral. No; but do you know when and where I *have* met with immorality in artists' circles?

Manders.   No, thank heaven, I don't!

Oswald.   Well, then, I shall have the pleasure of telling you. I have met with it when some one or other of your model husbands and fathers have come out there to have a bit of a look round on their own account, and have done the artists the honour of looking them up in their humble quarters. Then we had a chance of learning something, I can tell you. These gentlemen were able to instruct us about places and things that we had never so much as dreamt of.

Manders.   What? Do you want me to believe that honourable men when they get away from home will————

Oswald.   Have you never, when these same honourable men come home again, heard them deliver themselves on the subject of the prevalence of immorality abroad?

Manders.   Yes, of course, but————

Mrs. Alving.   I have heard them, too.

Oswald.   Well, you can take their word for it, unhesitatingly. Some of them are experts in the matter. *(Putting his hands to his head.)* To think that the glorious freedom of the beautiful life over there should be so besmirched!

Mrs. Alving.   You mustn't get too heated, Oswald; you gain nothing by that.

Oswald.   No, you are quite right, mother. Besides, it isn't good for me. It's because I am so infernally tired, you know. I will go out and

take a turn before dinner. I beg your pardon, Mr. Manders. It is impossible for you to realise the feeling; but it takes me that way.

[*Goes out by the farther door on the right.*]

Mrs. Alving.   My poor boy!

Manders.   You may well say so. This is what it has brought him to!
(MRS. ALVING *looks at him, but does not speak.*) He called himself the
prodigal son. It's only too true, alas—only too true! (MRS. ALVING *looks
steadily at him.*) And what do you say to all this?

Mrs. Alving.   I say that Oswald was right in every single word he said.

Manders.   Right? Right? To hold such principles as that?

Mrs. Alving.   In my loneliness here I have come to just the same
opinions as he, Mr. Manders. But I have never presumed to venture
upon such topics in conversation. Now there is no need; my boy shall
speak for me.

Manders.   You deserve the deepest pity, Mrs. Alving. It is my duty
to say an earnest word to you. It is no longer your business man and adviser, no longer your old friend and your dead husband's old friend,
that stands before you now. It is your priest that stands before you, just
as he did once at the most critical moment of your life.

Mrs. Alving.   And what is it that my priest has to say to me?

Manders.   First of all I must stir your memory. The moment is well
chosen. To-morrow is the tenth anniversary of your husband's death; to-
morrow the memorial to the departed will be unveiled; to-morrow I
shall speak to the whole assembly that will be met together. But to-day
I want to speak to you alone.

Mrs. Alving.   Very well, Mr. Manders, speak!

Manders.   Have you forgotten that after barely a year of married life
you were standing at the very edge of a precipice?—that you forsook
your house and home?—that you ran away from your husband—yes,
Mrs. Alving, ran away, ran away—and refused to return to him in spite
of his requests and entreaties?

Mrs. Alving.   Have you forgotten how unspeakably unhappy I was
during that first year?

Manders.   To crave for happiness in this world is simply to be possessed by a spirit of revolt. What right have we to happiness? No! we
must do our duty, Mrs. Alving. And your duty was to cleave to the man
you had chosen and to whom you were bound by a sacred bond.

Mrs. Alving.   You know quite well what sort of a life my husband
was living at that time—what excesses he was guilty of.

Manders.   I know only too well what rumour used to say of him;

and I should be the last person to approve of his conduct as a young
man, supposing that rumour spoke the truth. But it is not a wife's part
to be her husband's judge. You should have considered it your
bounden duty humbly to have borne the cross that a higher will had
laid upon you. But, instead of that, you rebelliously cast off your cross,
you deserted the man whose stumbling footsteps you should have sup-
ported, you did what was bound to imperil your good name and reputation, and came very near to imperilling the reputation of others into
the bargain.

Mrs. Alving.   Of others? Of one other, you mean.

Manders.   It was the height of imprudence, your seeking refuge
with me.

Mrs. Alving.   With our priest? With our intimate friend?

Manders.   All the more on that account. You should thank God
that I possessed the necessary strength of mind—that I was able to turn
you from your outrageous intention, and that it was vouchsafed to me
to succeed in leading you back into the path of duty and back to your
lawful husband.

Mrs. Alving.   Yes, Mr. Manders, that certainly was your doing.

Manders.   I was but the humble instrument of a higher power. And
is it not true that my having been able to bring you again under the
yoke of duty and obedience sowed the seeds of a rich blessing on all the
rest of your life? Did things not turn out as I foretold to you? Did not
your husband turn from straying in the wrong path as a man should?
Did he not, after all, live a life of love and good report with you all his
days? Did he not become a benefactor to the neighbourhood? Did he
not so raise you up to his level, so that by degrees you became his fellow-worker in all his undertakings—and a noble fellow-worker, too, I
know, Mrs. Alving; that praise I will give you.—But now I come to the
second serious false step in your life.

Mrs. Alving.   What do you mean?

Manders.   Just as once you forsook your duty as a wife, so, since
then, you have forsaken your duty as a mother.

Mrs. Alving.   Oh———!

Manders.   You have been overmastered all your life by a disastrous
spirit of wilfulness. All your impulses have led you towards what is
undisciplined and lawless. You have never been willing to submit to
any restraint. Anything in life that has seemed irksome to you, you have
thrown aside recklessly and unscrupulously, as if it were a burden that
you were free to rid yourself of if you would. It did not please you to be

a wife any longer, and so you left your husband. Your duties as a mother wire irksome to you, so you sent your child away among strangers.

Mrs. Alving. Yes, that is true; I did that.

Manders. And that is why you have become a stranger to him.

Mrs. Alving. No, no, I am not that!

Manders. You are; you must be. And what sort of a son is it that you have got back? Think over it seriously, Mrs. Alving. You erred grievously in your husband's case—you acknowledge as much, by erecting this memorial to him. Now you are bound to acknowledge how much you have erred in your son's case; possibly there may still be time to reclaim him from the paths of wickedness. Turn over a new leaf, and set yourself to reform what there may still be that is capable of reformation in him. Because *(with uplifted forefinger)* in very truth, Mrs. Alving, you are a guilty mother!—That is what I have thought it my duty to say to you.

[*A short silence.*]

Mrs. Alving (speaking slowly and with self-control). You have had your say, Mr. Manders, and to-morrow you will be making a public speech in memory of my husband. I shall not speak to-morrow. But now I wish to speak to you for a little, just as you have been speaking to me.

Manders. By all means; no doubt you wish to bring forward some excuses for your behaviour——

Mrs. Alving. No. I only want to tell you something.

Manders. Well?

Mrs. Alving. In all that you said just now about me and my husband, and about our life together after you had, as you put it, led me back into the path of duty—there was nothing that you knew at first hand. From that moment you never again set foot in our house—you, who had been our daily companion before that.

Manders. Remember that you and your husband moved out of town immediately afterwards.

Mrs. Alving. Yes, and you never once came out here to see us in my husband's lifetime. It was only the business in connection with the Orphanage that obliged you to come and see me.

Manders (in a low and uncertain voice). Helen—if that is a reproach, I can only beg you to consider——

Mrs. Alving. ——the respect you owed to your calling?—yes. All the more as I was a wife who had tried to run away from her husband. One can never be too careful to have nothing to do with such reckless women.

Manders. My dear—Mrs. Alving, you are exaggerating dread-fully———

Mrs. Alving. Yes, yes,—very well. What I mean is this, that when you condemn my conduct as a wife you have nothing more to go upon than ordinary public opinion.

Manders. I admit it. What then?

Mrs. Alving. Well—now, Mr. Manders, now I am going to tell you the truth. I had sworn to myself that you should know it one day—you, and you only!

Manders. And what may the truth be?

Mrs. Alving. The truth is this, that my husband died just as great a profligate as he had been all his life.

Manders (feeling for a chair). What are you saying?

Mrs. Alving. After nineteen years of married life, just as profli-gate—in his desires at all events—as he was before you married us.

Manders. And can you talk of his youthful indiscretions—his ir-regularities—his excesses, if you like—as a profligate life!

Mrs. Alving. That was what the doctor who attended him called it.

Manders. I don't understand what you mean.

Mrs. Alving. It is not necessary you should.

Manders. It makes my brain reel. To think that your marriage—all the years of wedded life you spent with your husband—were nothing but a hidden abyss of misery.

Mrs. Alving. That and nothing else. Now you know.

Manders. This—this bewilders me. I can't understand it! I can't grasp it! How in the world was it possible———? How could such a state of things remain concealed?

Mrs. Alving. That was just what I had to fight for incessantly, day after day. When Oswald was born, I thought I saw a slight improve-ment. But it didn't last long. And after that I had to fight doubly hard—fight a desperate fight so that no one should know what sort of a man my child's father was. You know quite well what an attractive manner he had; it seemed as if people could believe nothing but good of him. He was one of those men whose mode of life seems to have no effect upon their reputations. But at last, Mr. Manders—you must hear this too—at last something happened more abominable than everything else.

Manders. More abominable than what you have told me!

Mrs. Alving. I had borne with it all, though I knew only too well what he indulged in in secret, when he was out of the house. But when it came to the point of the scandal coming within our four walls———

Manders. Can you mean it! Here?

Mrs. Alving. Yes, here, in our own home. It was in there (*pointing to the nearer door on the right*) in the dining-room that I got the first hint of it. I had something to do in there and the door was standing ajar. I heard our maid come up from the garden with water for the flowers in the conservatory.

Manders. Well———?

Mrs. Alving. Shortly afterwards I heard my husband come in too. I heard him say something to her in a low voice. And then I heard— (*with a short laugh*)—oh, it rings in my ears still, with its mixture of what was heartbreaking and what was so ridiculous—I heard my own servant whisper: "Let me go, Mr. Alving! Let me be!"

Manders. What unseemly levity on his part! But surely nothing more than levity, Mrs. Alving, believe me.

Mrs. Alving. I soon knew what to believe. My husband had his will of the girl—and that intimacy had consequences, Mr. Manders.

Manders (as if turned to stone). And all that in this house! In this house!

Mrs. Alving. I have suffered a good deal in this house. To keep him at home in the evening—and at night—I have had to play the part of boon companion in his secret drinking-bouts in his room up there. I have had to sit there alone with him, have had to hobnob and drink with him, have had to listen to his ribald senseless talk, have had to fight with brute force to get him to bed———

Manders (trembling). And you were able to endure all this!

Mrs. Alving. I had my little boy, and endured it for his sake. But when the crowning insult came—when my own servant—then I made up my mind that there should be an end of it. I took the upper hand in the house, absolutely—both with him and all the others. I had a weapon to use against him, you see; he didn't dare to speak. It was then that Oswald was sent away. He was about seven then, and was beginning to notice things and ask questions as children will. I could endure all that, my friend. It seemed to me that the child would be poisoned if he breathed the air of this polluted house. That was why I sent him away. And now you understand, too, why he never set foot here as long as his father was alive. No one knows what it meant to me.

Manders. You have indeed had a pitiable experience.

Mrs. Alving. I could never have gone through with it, if I had not had my work. Indeed, I can boast that I have worked. All the increase in the value of the property, all the improvements, all the useful arrangements that my husband got the honour and glory of—do you suppose that he troubled himself about any of them? He, who used to lie the whole day on the sofa reading old Official Lists! No, you may as well know that too. It was I that kept him up to the mark when he had his lucid intervals; it was I that had to bear the whole burden of it when he began his excesses again or took to whining about his miserable condition.

Manders.   And this is the man you are building a memorial to!

Mrs. Alving.   There you see the power of an uneasy conscience.

Manders.   An uneasy conscience? What do you mean?

Mrs. Alving.   I had always before me the fear that it was impossible that the truth should not come out and be believed. That is why the Orphanage is to exist, to silence all rumours and clear away all doubt.

Manders.   You certainly have not fallen short of the mark in that, Mrs. Alving.

Mrs. Alving.   I had another very good reason. I did not wish Oswald, my own son, to inherit a penny that belonged to his father.

Manders.   Then it is with Mr. Alving's property———

Mrs. Alving.   Yes. The sums of money that, year after year, I have given towards this Orphanage, make up the amount of property—I have reckoned it carefully—which in the old days made Lieutenant Alving a catch.

Manders.   I understand.

Mrs. Alving.   That was my purchase money. I don't wish it to pass into Oswald's hands. My son shall have everything from me, I am determined.

[OSWALD *comes in by the farther door on the right. He has left his hat and coat outside.*]

Mrs. Alving.   Back again, my own dear boy?

Oswald.   Yes, what can one do outside in this everlasting rain? I hear dinner is nearly ready. That's good!

[REGINA *comes in from the dining-room, carrying a parcel.*]

Regina.   This parcel has come for you, ma'am.

[*Gives it to her.*]

Mrs. Alving (glancing at MANDERS).   The ode to be sung to-morrow, I expect.

Manders.   Hm———!

Regina. And dinner is ready.

Mrs. Alving. Good. We will come in a moment. I will just—*(begins to open the parcel).*

Regina (to OSWALD*).* Will you drink white or red wine, sir?

Oswald. Both, Miss Engstrand.

Regina. Bien—very good, Mr. Alving.

[*Goes into the dining-room.*]

Oswald. I may as well help you to uncork it————.

[*Follows her into the dining-room, leaving the door ajar after him.*]

Mrs. Alving. Yes, I thought so. Here is the ode, Mr. Manders.

Manders (clasping his hands). How shall I ever have the courage to-morrow to speak the address that————

Mrs. Alving. Oh, you will get through it.

Manders (in a low voice, fearing to be heard in the dining-room). Yes, we must raise no suspicions.

Mrs. Alving (quietly but firmly). No; and then this long dreadful comedy will be at an end. After to-morrow, I shall feel as if my dead husband had never lived in this house. There will be no one else here then but my boy and his mother.

[*From the dining-room is heard the noise of a chair falling; then* REGINA'S *voice is heard in a loud whisper:* Oswald! Are you mad? Let me go!]

Mrs. Alving (starting in horror). Oh————!

[*She stares wildly at the half-open door.* OSWALD *is heard coughing and humming, then the sound of a bottle being uncorked.*]

Manders (in an agitated manner). What's the matter? What is it, Mrs. Alving?

Mrs. Alving (hoarsely). Ghosts. The couple in the conservatory—over again.

Manders. What are you saying! Regina————? Is she————?

Mrs. Alving. Yes. Come. Not a word————!

[*Grips* MANDERS *by the arm and walks unsteadily with him into the dining-room.*]

ACT II

The same scene. The landscape is still obscured by mist. MANDERS *and* MRS. ALVING *come in from the dining-room.*

Mrs. Alving (*calls into the dining-room from the door-way*). Aren't you coming in here, Oswald?

Oswald. No, thanks; I think I will go out for a bit.

Mrs. Alving. Yes, do; the weather is clearing a little. (*She shuts the dining-room door, then goes to the hall door and calls.*) Regina!

Regina (*from without*). Yes, ma'am?

Mrs. Alving. Go down into the laundry and help with the garlands.

Regina. Yes, ma'am.

[MRS. ALVING *satisfies herself that she has gone, then shuts the door.*]

Manders. I suppose he can't hear us?

Mrs. Alving. Not when the door is shut. Besides, he is going out.

Manders. I am still quite bewildered. I don't know how I managed to swallow a mouthful of your excellent dinner.

Mrs. Alving (*walking up and down, and trying to control her agitation*). Nor I. But what are we to do?

Manders. Yes, what are we to do? Upon my word I don't know; I am so completely unaccustomed to things of this kind.

Mrs. Alving. I am convinced that nothing serious has happened yet.

Manders. Heaven forbid! But it is most unseemly behaviour, for all that.

Mrs. Alving. It is nothing more than a foolish jest of Oswald's, you may be sure.

Manders. Well, of course, as I said, I am quite inexperienced in such matters; but it certainly seems to me———

Mrs. Alving. Out of the house she shall go—and at once. That part of it is as clear as daylight———

Manders. Yes, that is quite clear.

Mrs. Alving. But where is she to go? We should not be justified in———

Manders. Where to? Home to her father, of course.

Mrs. Alving. To whom, did you say?

26

Manders. To her———. No, of course Engstrand isn't———. But, great heavens, Mrs. Alving, how is such a thing possible? You surely may have been mistaken, in spite of everything.

Mrs. Alving. There was no chance of mistake, more's the pity. Joanna was obliged to confess it to me—and my husband couldn't deny it. So there was nothing else to do but to hush it up.

Manders. No, that was the only thing to do.

Mrs. Alving. The girl was sent away at once, and was given a tolerably liberal sum to hold her tongue. She looked after the rest herself when she got to town. She renewed an old acquaintance with the carpenter Engstrand; gave him a hint, I suppose, of how much money she had got, and told him some fairy tale about a foreigner who had been here in his yacht in the summer. So she and Engstrand were married in a great hurry. Why, you married them yourself!

Manders. I can't understand it———. I remember clearly Engstrand's coming to arrange about the marriage. He was full of contrition, and accused himself bitterly for the light conduct he and his fiancée had been guilty of.

Mrs. Alving. Of course he had to take the blame on himself.

Manders. But the deceitfulness of it! And with me, too! I positively would not have believed it of Jacob Engstrand. I shall most certainly give him a serious talking to.—And the immorality of such a marriage! Simply for the sake of the money———! What sum was it that the girl had?

Mrs. Alving. It was seventy pounds.

Manders. Just think of it—for a paltry seventy pounds to let yourself be bound in marriage to a fallen woman!

Mrs. Alving. What about myself, then?—I let myself be bound in marriage to a fallen man.

Manders. Heaven forgive you! What are you saying? A fallen man?

Mrs. Alving. Do you suppose my husband was any purer, when I went with him to the altar, than Joanna was when Engstrand agreed to marry her?

Manders. The two cases are as different as day from night———

Mrs. Alving. Not so very different, after all. It is true there was a great difference in the price paid, between a paltry seventy pounds and a whole fortune.

Manders. How can you compare such totally different things! I presume you consulted your own heart—and your relations.

Mrs. Alving (looking away from him).   I thought you understood where what you call my heart had strayed to at that time.

Manders (in a constrained voice).   If I had understood anything of the kind, I would not have been a daily guest in your husband's house.

Mrs. Alving.   Well, at any rate this much is certain, that I didn't consult myself in the matter at all.

Manders.   Still you consulted those nearest to you, as was only right—your mother, your two aunts.

Mrs. Alving.   Yes, that is true. The three of them settled the whole matter for me. It seems incredible to me now, how clearly they made out that it would be sheer folly to reject such an offer. If my mother could only see what all that fine prospect has led to!

Manders.   No one can be responsible for the result of it. Anyway, there is this to be said, that the match was made in complete conformity with law and order.

Mrs. Alving (going to the window).   Oh, law and order! I often think it is that that is at the bottom of all the misery in the world.

Manders.   Mrs. Alving, it is very wicked of you to say that.

Mrs. Alving.   That may be so; but I don't attach importance to those obligations and considerations any longer. I cannot! I must struggle for my freedom.

Manders.   What do you mean?

Mrs. Alving (tapping on the window panes).   I ought never to have concealed what sort of a life my husband led. But I had not the courage to do otherwise then—for my own sake, either. I was too much of a coward.

Manders.   A coward?

Mrs. Alving.   If others had known anything of what happened, they would have said: "Poor man, it is natural enough that he should go astray, when he has a wife that has run away from him."

Manders.   They would have had a certain amount of justification for saying so.

Mrs. Alving (looking fixedly at him).   If I had been the woman I ought, I would have taken Oswald into my confidence and said to him: "Listen, my son, your father was a dissolute man"——

Manders.   Miserable woman——

Mrs. Alving.   ——and I would have told him all I have told you, from beginning to end.

Manders.   I am almost shocked at you, Mrs. Alving.

Mrs. Alving.   I know. I know quite well! I am shocked at myself

when I think of it. (*Comes away from the window.*) I am coward enough
for that.

Manders.   Can you call it cowardice that you simply did your duty!
Have you forgotten that a child should love and honour his father and
mother?

Mrs. Alving.   Don't let us talk in such general terms. Suppose we
say: "Ought Oswald to love and honour Mr. Alving?"

Manders.   You are a mother—isn't there a voice in your heart that
forbids you to shatter your son's ideals?

Mrs. Alving.   And what about the truth?

Manders.   What about his ideals?

Mrs. Alving.   Oh—ideals, ideals! If only I were not such a coward
as I am!

Manders.   Do not spurn ideals, Mrs. Alving—they have a way of
avenging themselves cruelly. Take Oswald's own case, now. He hasn't
many ideals, more's the pity. But this much I have seen, that his father
is something of an ideal to him.

Mrs. Alving.   You are right there.

Manders.   And his conception of his father is what you inspired and
encouraged by your letters.

Mrs. Alving.   Yes, I was swayed by duty and consideration for others; that was why I lied to my son, year in and year out. Oh, what a coward—what a coward I have been!

Manders.   You have built up a happy illusion in your son's mind,
Mrs. Alving—and that is a thing you certainly ought not to undervalue.

Mrs. Alving.   Ah, who knows if that is such a desirable thing after
all!—But anyway I don't intend to put up with any goings on with
Regina. I am not going to let him get the poor girl into trouble.

Manders.   Good heavens, no—that would be a frightful thing!

Mrs. Alving.   If only I knew whether he meant it seriously, and
whether it would mean happiness for him————

Manders.   In what way? I don't understand.

Mrs. Alving.   But that is impossible; Regina is not equal to it, unfortunately.

Manders.   I don't understand. What do you mean?

Mrs. Alving.   If I were not such a miserable coward, I would say to
him: "Marry her, or make any arrangement you like with her—only let
there be no deceit in the matter."

Manders.   Heaven forgive you! Are you actually suggesting anything so abominable, so unheard of, as a marriage between them!

Mrs. Alving. Unheard of, do you call it? Tell me honestly, Mr. Manders, don't you suppose there are plenty of married couples out here in the country that are just as nearly related as they are?

Manders. I am sure I don't understand you.

Mrs. Alving. Indeed you do.

Manders. I suppose you are thinking of cases where possibly————. It is only too true, unfortunately, that family life is not always as stainless as it should be. But as for the sort of thing you hint at—well, it's impossible to tell, at all events with any certainty. Here, on the other hand—for you, a mother, to be willing to allow your————

Mrs. Alving. But I am not willing to allow it. I would not allow it for anything in the world; that is just what I was saying.

Manders. No, because you are a coward, as you put it. But, supposing you were not a coward————! Great heavens—such a revolting union!

Mrs. Alving. Well, for the matter of that, we are all descended from a union of that description, so we are told. And who was it that was responsible for this state of things, Mr. Manders.?

Manders. I can't discuss such questions with you, Mrs. Alving; you are by no means in the right frame of mind for that. But for you to dare to say that it is cowardly of you————!

Mrs. Alving. I will tell you what I mean by that. I am frightened and timid, because I am obsessed by the presence of ghosts that I never can get rid of.

Manders. The presence of what?

Mrs. Alving. Ghosts. When I heard Regina and Oswald in there, it was just like seeing ghosts before my eyes. I am half inclined to think we are all ghosts, Mr. Manders. It is not only what we have inherited from our fathers and mothers that exists again in us, but all sorts of old dead ideas and all kinds of old dead beliefs and things of that kind. They are not actually alive in us; but there they are dormant, all the same, and we can never be rid of them. Whenever I take up a newspaper and read it, I fancy I see ghosts creeping between the lines. There must be ghosts all over the world. They must be as countless as the grains of the sands, it seems to me. And we are so miserably afraid of the light, all of us.

Manders. Ah!—there we have the outcome of your reading. Fine fruit it has borne—this abominable, subversive, free-thinking literature!

Mrs. Alving. You are wrong there, my friend. You are the one who made me begin to think; and I owe you my best thanks for it.

Manders. I!

Mrs. Alving. Yes, by forcing me to submit to what you called my duty and my obligations; by praising as right and just what my whole soul revolted against, as it would against something abominable. That was what led me to examine your teachings critically. I only wanted to unravel one point in them; but as soon as I had got that unravelled, the whole fabric came to pieces. And then I realised that it was only machine-made.

Manders (softly, and with emotion). Is that all I accomplished by the hardest struggle of my life?

Mrs. Alving. Call it rather the most ignominious defeat of your life.

Manders. It was the greatest victory of my life, Helen; victory over myself.

Mrs. Alving. It was a wrong done to both of us.

Manders. A wrong?—wrong for me to entreat you as a wife to go back to your lawful husband, when you came to me half distracted and crying: "Here I am, take me!" Was that a wrong?

Mrs. Alving. I think it was.

Manders. We two do not understand one another.

Mrs. Alving. Not now, at all events.

Manders. Never—even in my most secret thoughts—have I for a moment regarded you as anything but the wife of another.

Mrs. Alving. Do you believe what you say?

Manders. Helen————!

Mrs. Alving. One so easily forgets one's own feelings.

Manders. Not I. I am the same as I always was.

Mrs. Alving. Yes, yes—don't let us talk any more about the old days. You are buried up to your eyes now in committees and all sorts of business; and I am here, fighting with ghosts both without and within me.

Manders. I can at all events help you to get the better of those without you. After all that I have been horrified to hear from you to-day, I cannot conscientiously allow a young defenceless girl to remain in your house.

Mrs. Alving. Don't you think it would be best if we could get her settled?—by some suitable marriage, I mean.

Manders. Undoubtedly. I think, in any case, it would have been desirable for her. Regina is at an age now that—well, I don't know much about these things, but————

Mrs. Alving. Regina developed very early.

Manders. Yes, didn't she. I fancy I remember thinking she was re- markably well developed, bodily, at the time I prepared her for Confirmation. But, for the time being, she must in any case go home. Under her father's care—no, but of course Engstrand is not————. To think that he, of all men, could so conceal the truth from me!

[*A knock is heard at the hall door.*]

Mrs. Alving. Who can that be? Come in!

[ENGSTRAND, *dressed in his Sunday clothes, appears in the door- way.*]

Engstrand. I humbly beg pardon, but————

Manders. Aha! Hm!————

Mrs. Alving. Oh, it's you, Engstrand!

Engstrand. There were none of the maids about, so I took the great liberty of knocking.

Mrs. Alving. That's all right. Come in. Do you want to speak to me?

Engstrand (coming in). No, thank you very much, ma'm. It was Mr. Manders I wanted to speak to for a moment.

Manders (walking up and down). Hm!—do you. You want to speak to me, do you?

Engstrand. Yes, sir, I wanted so very much to————

Manders (stopping in front of him). Well, may I ask what it is you want?

Engstrand. It's this way, Mr. Manders. We are being paid off now. And many thanks to you, Mrs. Alving. And now the work is quite fin- ished, I thought it would be so nice and suitable if all of us, who have worked so honestly together all this time, were to finish up with a few prayers this evening.

Manders. Prayers? Up at the Orphanage?

Engstrand. Yes, sir, but if it isn't agreeable to you, then————

Manders. Oh, certainly———— but—hm!————

Engstrand. I have made a practice of saying a few prayers there my- self each evening————

Mrs. Alving. Have you?

Engstrand. Yes, ma'am, now and then—just as a little edification, so to speak. But I am only a poor common man, and haven't rightly the gift, alas—and so I thought that as Mr. Manders happened to be here, perhaps————

Manders. Look here, Engstrand. First of all I must ask you a question. Are you in a proper frame of mind for such a thing? Is your conscience free and untroubled?

Engstrand. Heaven have mercy on me a sinner! My conscience isn't worth our speaking about, Mr. Manders.

Manders. But it is just what we must speak about. What do you say to my question?

Engstrand. My conscience? Well—it's uneasy sometimes, of course.

Manders. Ah, you admit that at all events. Now will you tell me, without any concealment—what is your relationship to Regina?

Mrs. Alving (hastily). Mr. Manders!

Manders (calming her). —Leave it to me!

Engstrand. With Regina? Good Lord, how you frightened me! *(Looks at* Mrs. Alving.*)* There is nothing wrong with Regina, is there?

Manders. Let us hope not. What I want to know is, what is your relationship to her? You pass as her father, don't you?

Engstrand (unsteadily). Well—hm!—you know, sir, what happened between me and my poor Joanna.

Manders. No more distortion of the truth! Your late wife made a full confession to Mrs. Alving, before she left her service.

Engstrand. What!—do you mean to say——? Did she do that after all?

Manders. You see it has all come out, Engstrand.

Engstrand. Do you mean to say that she, who gave me her promise and solemn oath——

Manders. Did she take an oath?

Engstrand. Well, no—she only gave me her word, but as seriously as a woman could.

Manders. And all these years you have been hiding the truth from me—from me, who have had such complete and absolute faith in you.

Engstrand. I am sorry to say I have, sir.

Manders. Did I deserve that from you, Engstrand? Haven't I been always ready to help you in word and deed as far as lay in my power? Answer me! Is it not so?

Engstrand. Indeed there's many a time I should have been very badly off without you, sir.

Manders. And this is the way you repay me—by causing me to make false entries in the church registers, and afterwards keeping back from me for years the information which you owed it both to me and to your sense of the truth to divulge. Your conduct has been absolutely inexcusable, Engstrand, and from to-day everything is at an end be-tween us.

Engstrand (with a sigh).   Yes, I can see that's what it means.

Manders.   Yes, because how can you possibly justify what you did?

Engstrand.   Was the poor girl to go and increase her load of shame by talking about it? Just suppose, sir, for a moment that your reverence was in the same predicament as my poor Joanna———

Manders.   I!

Engstrand.   Good Lord, sir, I don't mean the same predicament. I mean, suppose there were something your reverence were ashamed of in the eyes of the world, so to speak. We men oughtn't to judge a poor woman too hardly, Mr. Manders.

Manders.   But I am not doing so at all. It is you I am blaming.

Engstrand.   Will your reverence grant me leave to ask you a small question?

Manders.   Ask away.

Engstrand.   Shouldn't you say it was right for a man to raise up the fallen?

Manders.   Of course it is.

Engstrand.   And isn't a man bound to keep his word of honour?

Manders.   Certainly he is; but———

Engstrand.   At the time when Joanna had her misfortune with this Englishman—or maybe he was an American or a Russian, as they call 'em—well, sir, then she came to town. Poor thing, she had refused me once or twice before; she only had eyes for good-looking men in those days, and I had this crooked leg then. Your reverence will remember how I had ventured up into a dancing-saloon where seafaring men were revelling in drunkenness and intoxication, as they say. And when I tried to exhort them to turn from their evil ways———

Mrs. Alving (coughs from the window).   Ahem!

Manders.   I know, Engstrand, I know—the rough brutes threw you downstairs. You have told me about that incident before. The affliction to your leg is a credit to you.

Engstrand.   I don't want to claim credit for it, your reverence. But what I wanted to tell you was that she came then and confided in me with tears and gnashing of teeth. I can tell you, sir, it went to my heart to hear her.

Manders.   Did it, indeed, Engstrand? Well, what then?

Engstrand.   Well, then I said to her: "The American is roaming about on the high seas, he is. And you, Joanna," I said, "you have committed a sin and are a fallen woman. But here stands Jacob Engstrand," I said, "on two strong legs"—of course that was only speaking in a kind of metaphor, as it were, your reverence.

Manders. I quite understand. Go on.

Engstrand. Well, sir, that was how I rescued her and made her my lawful wife, so that no one should know how recklessly she had carried on with the stranger.

Manders. That was all very kindly done. The only thing I cannot justify was your bringing yourself to accept the money———

Engstrand. Money? I? Not a farthing.

Manders (to Mrs. Alving, *in a questioning tone).* But———

Engstrand. Ah, yes!—wait a bit; I remember now. Joanna did have a trifle of money, you are quite right. But I didn't want to know anything about that. "Fie," I said, "on the mammon of unrighteousness, it's the price of your sin; as for this tainted gold"—or notes, or whatever it was—"we will throw it back in the American's face," I said. But he had gone away and disappeared on the stormy seas, your reverence.

Manders. Was that how it was, my good fellow?

Engstrand. It was, sir. So then Joanna and I decided that the money should go towards the child's bringing-up, and that's what became of it; and I can give a faithful account of every single penny of it.

Manders. This alters the complexion of the affair very considerably.

Engstrand. That's how it was your reverence. And I make bold to say that I have been a good father to Regina—as far as was in my power—for I am a poor erring mortal, alas!

Manders. There, there, my dear Engstrand———

Engstrand. Yes, I do make bold to say that I brought up the child, and made my poor Joanna a loving and careful husband, as the Bible says we ought. But it never occurred to me to go to your reverence and claim credit for it or boast about it because I had done one good deed in this world. No; when Jacob Engstrand does a thing like that, he holds his tongue about it. Unfortunately it doesn't often happen, I know that only too well. And whenever I do come to see your reverence, I never seem to have anything but trouble and wickedness to talk about. Because, as I said just now—and I say it again—conscience can be very hard on us sometimes.

Manders. Give me your hand, Jacob Engstrand.

Engstrand. Oh, sir, I don't like———

Manders. No nonsense. *(Grasps his hand.)* That's it!

Engstrand. And may I make bold humbly to beg your reverence's pardon——

Manders. You? On the contrary it is for me to beg your pardon——

Engstrand. Oh no, sir.

Manders. Yes, certainly it is, and I do it with my whole heart. Forgive me for having so much misjudged you. And I assure you that if I can do anything for you to prove my sincere regret and my goodwill towards you——

Engstrand. Do you mean it, sir?

Manders. It would give me the greatest pleasure.

Engstrand. As a matter of fact, sir, you could do it now. I am thinking of using the honest money I have put away out of my wages up here, in establishing a sort of Sailors' Home in the town.

Mrs. Alving. You?

Engstrand. Yes, to be a sort of Refuge, as it were. There are such manifold temptations laying in wait for sailor men when they are roaming about on shore. But my idea is that in this house of mine they should have a sort of parental care looking after them.

Manders. What do you say to that, Mrs. Alving!

Engstrand. I haven't much to begin such a work with, I know; but Heaven might prosper it, and if I found any helping hand stretched out to me, then——

Manders. Quite so; we will talk over the matter further. Your project attracts me enormously. But in the meantime go back to the Orphanage and put everything tidy and light the lights, so that the occasion may seem a little solemn. And then we will spend a little edifying time together, my dear Engstrand, for now I am sure you are in a suitable frame of mind.

Engstrand. I believe I am, sir, truly. Good-bye, then, Mrs. Alving, and thank you for all your kindness; and take good care of Regina for me. *(Wipes a tear from his eye.)* Poor Joanna's child—it is an extraordinary thing, but she seems to have grown into my life and to hold me by the heartstrings. That's how I feel about it, truly.

[*Bows and goes out.*]

Manders. Now then, what do you think of him, Mrs. Alving! That was quite another explanation that he gave us.

Mrs. Alving. It was, indeed.

Manders. There, you see how exceedingly careful we ought to be in condemning our fellow-men. But at the same time it gives one genuine pleasure to find that one was mistaken. Don't you think so?

Mrs. Alving. What I think is that you are, and always will remain, a big baby, Mr. Manders.

Manders. I?

Mrs. Alving (laying her hands on his shoulders). And I think that I should like very much to give you a good hug.

Manders (drawing back hastily). No, no, good gracious! What an idea!

Mrs. Alving (with a smile). Oh, you needn't be afraid of me.

Manders (standing by the table). You choose such an extravagant way of expressing yourself sometimes. Now I must get these papers together and put them in my bag. *(Does so.)* That's it. And now good-bye, for the present. Keep your eyes open when Oswald comes back. I will come back and see you again presently.

> [*He takes his hat and goes out by the hall door.* MRS. ALVING *sighs, glances out of the window, puts one or two things tidy in the room and turns to go into the dining-room. She stops in the doorway with a stifled cry.*]

Mrs. Alving. Oswald, are you still sitting at table!

Oswald (from the dining-room). I am only finishing my cigar.

Mrs. Alving. I thought you had gone out for a little turn.

Oswald (from within the room). In weather like this? *(A glass is heard clinking.* MRS. ALVING *leaves the door open and sits down with her knitting on the couch by the window.)* Wasn't that Mr. Manders that went out just now?

Mrs. Alving. Yes, he has gone over to the Orphanage.

Oswald. Oh.

> [*The clink of a bottle on a glass is heard again.*]

Mrs. Alving (with an uneasy expression). Oswald, dear, you should be careful with that liqueur. It is strong.

Oswald. It's a good protective against the damp.

Mrs. Alving. Wouldn't you rather come in here?

Oswald. You know you don't like smoking in there.

Mrs. Alving. You may smoke a cigar in here, certainly.

Oswald. All right; I will come in, then. Just one drop more. There! *(Comes in, smoking a cigar, and shuts the door after him. A short silence.)* Where has the parson gone?

Mrs. Alving. I told you he had gone over to the Orphanage.

Oswald. Oh, so you did.

Mrs. Alving. You shouldn't sit so long at table, Oswald.

Oswald (holding his cigar behind his back). But it's so nice and

cosy, mother dear. (*Caresses her with one hand.*) Think what it means
to me—to have come home; to sit at my mother's own table, in my
mother's own room, and to enjoy the charming meals she gives me.

Mrs. Alving.   My dear, dear boy!

Oswald (*a little impatiently, as he walks up and down smoking.*)
And what else is there for me to do here? I have no occupation———

Mrs. Alving.   No occupation?

Oswald.   Not in this ghastly weather, when there isn't a blink of
sunshine all day long. (*Walks up and down the floor.*) Not to be able to
work, it's———!

Mrs. Alving.   I don't believe you were wise to come home.

Oswald.   Yes, mother; I had to.

Mrs. Alving.   Because I would ten times rather give up the happiness of having you with me, sooner than that you should———

Oswald (*standing still by the table*).   Tell me, mother—is it really
such a great happiness for you to have me at home?

Mrs. Alving.   Can you ask?

Oswald (*crumpling up a newspaper*).   I should have thought it
would have been pretty much the same to you whether I were here or
away.

Mrs. Alving.   Have you the heart to say that to your mother,
Oswald?

Oswald.   But you have been quite happy living without me so far.

Mrs. Alving.   Yes, I have lived without you—that is true.

  [*A silence. The dusk falls by degrees.* OSWALD *walks restlessly up
    and down. He has laid aside his cigar.*]

Oswald (*stopping beside* MRS. ALVING).   Mother, may I sit on the
couch beside you?

Mrs. Alving.   Of course, my dear boy.

Oswald (*sitting down*).   Now I must tell you something, mother.

Mrs. Alving (*anxiously*).   What?

Oswald (*staring in front of him*).   I can't bear it any longer.

Mrs. Alving.   Bear what? What do you mean?

Oswald (*as before*).   I couldn't bring myself to write to you about it;
and since I have been at home———

Mrs. Alving (*catching him by the arm*).   Oswald, what is it?

Oswald.   Both yesterday and to-day I have tried to push my
thoughts away from me—to free myself from them. But I can't.

Mrs. Alving (*getting up*).   You must speak plainly, Oswald!

Oswald (*drawing her down to her seat again*).   Sit still, and I will try

and tell you. I have made a great deal of the fatigue I felt after my journey———

Mrs. Alving. Well, what of that?

Oswald. But that isn't what is the matter. It is no ordinary fatigue———

Mrs. Alving (trying to get up). You are not ill, Oswald!

Oswald (pulling her down again). Sit still, mother. Do take it quietly. I am not exactly ill—not ill in the usual sense. *(Takes his head in
his hands.)* Mother, it's my mind that has broken down—gone to
pieces—I shall never be able to work any more!

> [*Buries his face in his hands and throws himself at her knees in an
> outburst of sobs.*]

Mrs. Alving (pale and trembling). Oswald! Look at me! No, no, it
isn't true!

Oswald (looking up with a distracted expression). Never to be able
to work any more! Never—never! A living death! Mother, can you
imagine anything so horrible!

Mrs. Alving. My poor unhappy boy? How has this terrible thing
happened?

Oswald (sitting up again). That is just what I cannot possibly understand. I have never lived recklessly, in any sense. You must believe
that of me, mother! I have never done that.

Mrs. Alving. I haven't a doubt of it, Oswald.

Oswald. And yet this comes upon me all the same!—this terrible
disaster!

Mrs. Alving. Oh, but it will all come right again, my dear precious
boy. It is nothing but overwork. Believe me, that is so.

Oswald (dully). I thought so too, at first; but it isn't so.

Mrs. Alving. Tell me all about it.

Oswald. Yes, I will.

Mrs. Alving. When did you first feel anything?

Oswald. It was just after I had been home last time and had got
back to Paris. I began to feel the most violent pains in my head—mostly
at the back, I think. It was as if a tight band of iron was pressing on me
from my neck upwards.

Mrs. Alving. And then?

Oswald. At first I thought it was nothing but the headaches I always
used to be so much troubled with while I was growing.

Mrs. Alving. Yes, yes———

Oswald. But it wasn't; I soon saw that. I couldn't work any longer. I
would try and start some big new picture; but it seemed as if all my fac-

ulties had forsaken me, as if all my strength were paralysed. I couldn't manage to collect my thoughts; my head seemed to swim—everything went round and round. It was a horrible feeling! At last I sent for a doctor—and from him I learnt the truth.

Mrs. Alving. In what way do you mean?

Oswald. He was one of the best doctors there. He made me describe what I felt, and then he began to ask me a whole heap of questions which seemed to me to have nothing to do with the matter. I couldn't see what he was driving at———

Mrs. Alving. Well?

Oswald. At last he said: "You have had the canker of disease in you practically from your birth"—the actual word he used was "vermoulu."

Mrs. Alving (anxiously). What did he mean by that?

Oswald. I couldn't understand, either—and I asked him for a clearer explanation. And then the old cynic said—(clenching his fist). Oh!———

Mrs. Alving. What did he say?

Oswald. He said: "The sins of the fathers are visited on the children."

Mrs. Alving (getting up slowly). The sins of the fathers———!

Oswald. I nearly struck him in the face———

Mrs. Alving (walking across the room). The sins of the fathers———!

Oswald (smiling sadly). Yes, just imagine! Naturally I assured him that what he thought was impossible. But do you think he paid any heed to me? No, he persisted in his opinion; and it was only when I got out your letters and translated to him all the passages that referred to my father———

Mrs. Alving. Well, and then?

Oswald. Well, then of course he had to admit that he was on the wrong tack; and then I learnt the truth—the incomprehensible truth! I ought to have had nothing to do with the joyous happy life I had lived with my comrades. It had been too much for my strength. So it was my own fault!

Mrs. Alving. No, no, Oswald! Don't believe that!

Oswald. There was no other explanation of it possible, he said. That is the most horrible part of it. My whole life incurably ruined—just because of my own imprudence. All that I wanted to do in the world—not to dare to think of it any more—not to be *able* to think of it! Oh! if only I could live my life over again—if only I could undo what I have done!

[*Throws himself on his face on the couch.* MRS. ALVING *wrings her hands and walks up and down silently fighting with herself.*]

Oswald (*looks up after a while, raising himself on his elbows*). If only it had been something I had inherited—something I could not help. But, instead of that, to have disgracefully, stupidly, thoughtlessly thrown away one's happiness, one's health, everything in the world—one's future, one's life———

Mrs. Alving. No, no, my darling boy; that is impossible! (*Bending over him.*) Things are not so desperate as you think.

Oswald. Ah, you don't know———. (*Springs up.*) And to think, mother, that I should bring all this sorrow upon you! Many a time I have almost wished and hoped that you really did not care so very much for me.

Mrs. Alving. I, Oswald? My only son! All that I have in the world! The only thing I care about!

Oswald (*taking hold of her hands and kissing them*). Yes, yes, I know that is so. When I am at home I know that is true. And that is one of the hardest parts of it to me. But now you know all about it; and now we won't talk any more about it to-day. I can't stand thinking about it long at a time. (*Walks across the room.*) Let me have something to drink, mother!

Mrs. Alving. To drink? What do you want?

Oswald. Oh, anything you like. I suppose you have got some punch in the house.

Mrs. Alving. Yes, but my dear Oswald———!

Oswald. Don't tell me I mustn't, mother. Do be nice! I must have something to drown these gnawing thoughts. (*Goes into the conservatory.*) And how—how gloomy it is here! (MRS. ALVING *rings the bell.*) And this incessant rain. It may go on week after week—a whole month. Never a ray of sunshine. I don't remember ever having seen the sun shine once when I have been at home.

Mrs. Alving. Oswald—you are thinking of going away from me!

Oswald. Hm!—(*sighs deeply*). I am not thinking about anything. I *can't* think about anything! (*In a low voice.*) I have to let that alone.

Regina (*coming from the dining-room*). Did you ring, ma'am?

Mrs. Alving. Yes, let us have the lamp in.

Regina. In a moment, ma'am; it is already lit.

[*Goes out.*]

Mrs. Alving (*going up to* OSWALD). Oswald, don't keep anything back from me.

Oswald. I don't, mother. *(Goes to the table.)* It seems to me I have told you a good lot.

[REGINA *brings the lamp and puts it upon the table.*]

Mrs. Alving. Regina, you might bring us a small bottle of champagne.

Regina. Yes, ma'am.

[*Goes out.*]

Oswald (taking hold of his mother's face). That's right. I knew my mother wouldn't let her son go thirsty.

Mrs. Alving. My poor dear boy, how could I refuse you anything now?

Oswald (eagerly). Is that true, mother? Do you mean it?

Mrs. Alving. Mean what?

Oswald. That you couldn't deny me anything?

Mrs. Alving. My dear Oswald——

Oswald. Hush!

[REGINA *brings in a tray with a small bottle of champagne and two glasses, which she puts on the table.*]

Regina. Shall I open the bottle?

Oswald. No, thank you, I will do it.

[REGINA *goes out.*]

Mrs. Alving (sitting down at the table). What did you mean, when you asked if I could refuse you nothing?

Oswald (busy opening the bottle). Let us have a glass first—or two.

[*He draws the cork, fills one glass and is going to fill the other.*]

Mrs. Alving (holding her hand over the second glass). No, thanks—not for me.

Oswald. Oh, well, for me then!

[*He empties his glass, fills it again and empties it; then sits down at the table.*]

Mrs. Alving (expectantly). Now, tell me.

Oswald (without looking at her). Tell me this; I thought you and Mr. Manders seemed so strange—so quiet—at dinner.

Mrs. Alving. Did you notice that?

Oswald. Yes. Ahem! *(After a short pause.)* Tell me—What do you think of Regina?

Mrs. Alving. What do I think of her?

Oswald. Yes, isn't she splendid!

Mrs. Alving. Dear Oswald, you don't know her as well as I do———
Oswald. What of that?
Mrs. Alving. Regina was too long at home, unfortunately. I ought to have taken her under my charge sooner.
Oswald. Yes, but isn't she splendid to look at, mother?
[*Fills his glass.*]
Mrs. Alving. Regina has many serious faults———
Oswald. Yes, but what of that?
[*Drinks.*]
Mrs. Alving. But I am fond of her, all the same; and I have made myself responsible for her. I wouldn't for the world she should come to any harm.
Oswald (jumping up). Mother, Regina is my only hope of salvation!
Mrs. Alving (getting up). What do you mean?
Oswald. I can't go on bearing all this agony of mind alone.
Mrs. Alving. Haven't you your mother to help you to bear it?
Oswald. Yes, I thought so; that was why I came home to you. But it is no use; I see that it isn't. I cannot spend my life here.
Mrs. Alving. Oswald!
Oswald. I must live a different sort of life, mother; so I shall have to go away from you. I don't want you watching it.
Mrs. Alving. My unhappy boy! But, Oswald, as long as you are ill like this———
Oswald. If it was only a matter of feeling ill, I would stay with you, mother. You are the best friend I have in the world.
Mrs. Alving. Yes, I am that, Oswald, am I not?
Oswald (walking restlessly about). But all this torment—the regret, the remorse—and the deadly fear. Oh—this horrible fear!
Mrs. Alving (following him). Fear? Fear of what? What do you mean?
Oswald. Oh, don't ask me any more about it. I don't know what it is. I can't put it into words. (MRS. ALVING *crosses the room and rings the bell.*) What do you want?
Mrs. Alving. I want my boy to be happy, that's what I want. He mustn't brood over anything. (To REGINA, *who has come to the door.*) More champagne—a large bottle.
Oswald. Mother!
Mrs. Alving. Do you think we country people don't know how to live?

Oswald. Isn't she splendid to look at? What a figure! And the picture of health!

Mrs. Alving (sitting down at the table). Sit down, Oswald, and let us have a quiet talk.

Oswald (sitting down). You don't know, mother, that I owe Regina a little reparation.

Mrs. Alving. You!

Oswald. Oh, it was only a little thoughtlessness—call it what you like. Something quite innocent, anyway. The last time I was home——

Mrs. Alving. Yes?

Oswald. ——she used often to ask me questions about Paris, and I told her one thing and another about the life there. And I remember saying one day: "Wouldn't you like to go there yourself?"

Mrs. Alving. Well?

Oswald. I saw her blush, and she said: "Yes, I should like to very much." "All right," I said, "I daresay it might be managed"—or something of that sort.

Mrs. Alving. And then?

Oswald. I naturally had forgotten all about it; but the day before yesterday I happened to ask her if she was glad I was to be so long at home——

Mrs. Alving. Well?

Oswald. ——and she looked so queerly at me, and asked: "But what is to become of my trip to Paris?"

Mrs. Alving. Her trip!

Oswald. And then I got it out of her that she had taken the thing seriously, and had been thinking about me all the time, and had set herself to learn French——

Mrs. Alving. So that was why——

Oswald. Mother—when I saw this fine, splendid, handsome girl standing there in front of me—I had never paid any attention to her before then—but now, when she stood there as if with open arms ready for me to take her to myself——

Mrs. Alving. Oswald!

Oswald. ——then I realised that my salvation lay in her, for I saw the joy of life in her.

Mrs. Alving (starting back). The joy of life——? Is there salvation in that?

Regina (coming in from the dining-room with a bottle of champagne). Excuse me for being so long; but I had to go to the cellar.

[*Puts the bottle down on the table.*]

Oswald. Bring another glass, too.

Regina (looking at him in astonishment). The mistress's glass is there, sir.

Oswald. Yes, but fetch one for yourself, Regina. (REGINA *starts, and gives a quick shy glance at* MRS. ALVING.) Well?

Regina (in a low and hesitating voice). Do you wish me to, ma'am?

Mrs. Alving. Fetch the glass, Regina.

[REGINA *goes into the dining-room.*]

Oswald (looking after her). Have you noticed how well she walks?—so firmly and confidently!

Mrs. Alving. It cannot be, Oswald.

Oswald. It is settled. You must see that. It is no use forbidding it. (REGINA *comes in with a glass, which she holds in her hand.*) Sit down, Regina.

[REGINA *looks questioningly at* MRS. ALVING.]

Mrs. Alving. Sit down. (REGINA *sits down on a chair near the dining-room door, still holding the glass in her hand.*) Oswald, what was it you were saying about the joy of life?

Oswald. Ah, mother—the joy of life! You don't know very much about that at home here. I shall never realise it here.

Mrs. Alving. Not even when you are with me?

Oswald. Never at home. But you can't understand that.

Mrs. Alving. Yes, indeed I almost think I do understand you—now.

Oswald. That—and the joy of work. They are really the same thing at bottom. But you don't know anything about that either.

Mrs. Alving. Perhaps you are right. Tell me some more about it, Oswald.

Oswald. Well, all I mean is that here people are brought up to believe that work is a curse and a punishment for sin, and that life is a state of wretchedness and that the sooner we can get out of it the better.

Mrs. Alving. A vale of tears, yes. And we quite conscientiously make it so.

Oswald. But the people over there will have none of that. There is no one there who really believes doctrines of that kind any longer. Over there the mere fact of being alive is thought to be a matter for exultant happiness. Mother, have you noticed that everything I have painted has turned upon the joy of life?—always upon the joy of life, unfailingly. There is light there, and sunshine, and a holiday feeling—and people's faces beaming with happiness. That is why I am afraid to stay at home here with you.

Mrs. Alving. Afraid? What are you afraid of here, with me?

Oswald. I am afraid that all these feelings that are so strong in me would degenerate into something ugly here.

Mrs. Alving (looking steadily at him). Do you think that is what would happen?

Oswald. I am certain it would. Even if one lived the same life at home here, as over there—it would never really be the same life.

Mrs. Alving (who has listened anxiously to him, gets up with a thoughtful expression and says:) Now I see clearly how it all happened.

Oswald. What do you see?

Mrs. Alving. I see it now for the first time. And now I can speak.

Oswald (getting up). Mother, I don't understand you.

Regina (who has got up also). Perhaps I had better go.

Mrs. Alving. No, stay here. Now I can speak. Now, my son, you shall know the whole truth. Oswald! Regina!

Oswald. Hush!—here is the parson——

[MANDERS *comes in by the hall door.*]

Manders. Well, my friends, we have been spending an edifying time over there.

Oswald. So have we.

Manders. Engstrand must have help with his Sailors' Home. Regina must go home with him and give him her assistance.

Regina. No, thank you, Mr. Manders.

Manders (perceiving her for the first time). What——? you in here?—and with a wineglass in your hand!

Regina (putting down the glass hastily). I beg your pardon——!

Oswald. Regina is going away with me, Mr. Manders.

Manders. Going away! With you!

Oswald. Yes, as my wife—if she insists on that.

Manders. But, good heavens——!

Regina. It is not my fault, Mr. Manders.

Oswald. Or else she stays here if I stay.

Regina (involuntarily). Here!

Manders. I am amazed at you, Mrs. Alving.

Mrs. Alving. Neither of those things will happen, for now I can speak openly.

Manders. But you won't do that! No, no, no!

Mrs. Alving. Yes, I can and I will. And without destroying anyone's ideals.

Oswald. Mother, what is it that is being concealed from me?

Regina (listening). Mrs. Alving! Listen! They are shouting outside.

[*Goes into the conservatory and looks out.*]

Oswald (going to the window on the left). What can be the matter? Where does that glare come from?

Regina (calls out). The Orphanage is on fire!

Mrs. Alving (going to the window). On fire?

Manders. On fire? Impossible. I was there just a moment ago.

Oswald. Where is my hat? Oh, never mind that. Father's Orphanage——!

[*Runs out through the garden door.*]

Mrs. Alving. My shawl, Regina! The whole place is in flames.

Manders. How terrible! Mrs. Alving, that fire is a judgment on this house of sin!

Mrs. Alving. Quite so. Come, Regina.

[*She and* REGINA *hurry out.*]

Manders (clasping his hands). And no insurance!

[*Follows them out.*]

ACT III

*The same scene. All the doors are standing open. The lamp is still burn-
ing on the table. It is dark outside, except for a faint glimmer of light
seen through the windows at the back.* MRS. ALVING, *with a shawl
over her head, is standing in the conservatory, looking out.* REGINA,
also wrapped in a shawl, is standing a little behind her.

Mrs. Alving.   Everything burnt—down to the ground.

Regina.   It is burning still in the basement.

Mrs. Alving.   I can't think why Oswald doesn't come back. There is
no chance of saving anything.

Regina.   Shall I go and take his hat to him?

Mrs. Alving.   Hasn't he even got his hat?

Regina (pointing to the hall).   No, there it is, hanging up.

Mrs. Alving.   Never mind. He is sure to come back soon. I will go
and see what he is doing.

[*Goes out by the garden door.* MANDERS *comes in from the hall.*]

Manders.   Isn't Mrs. Alving here?

Regina.   She has just this moment gone down into the garden.

Manders.   I have never spent such a terrible night in my life.

Regina.   Isn't it a shocking misfortune, sir!

Manders.   Oh, don't speak about it. I scarcely dare to think about it.

Regina.   But how can it have happened?

Manders.   Don't ask me, Miss Engstrand! How should I know? Are
you going to suggest too———? Isn't it enough that your father———?

Regina.   What has he done?

Manders.   He has nearly driven me crazy.

Engstrand (coming in from the hall).   Mr. Manders———!

Manders (turning round with a start).   Have you even followed me
here!

Engstrand.   Yes, God help us all———! Great heavens! What a
dreadful thing, your reverence!

Manders (walking up and down).   Oh dear, oh dear!

Regina.   What do you mean?

Engstrand.   Our little prayer-meeting was the cause of it all, don't
you see? (*Aside, to* REGINA.) Now we've got the old fool, my girl.

48

(Aloud.) And to think it is my fault that Mr. Manders should be the cause of such a thing!

Manders.   I assure you, Engstrand———

Engstrand.   But there was no one else carrying a light there except you, sir.

Manders (standing still).   Yes, so you say. But I have no clear recollection of having had a light in my hand.

Engstrand.   But I saw quite distinctly your reverence take a candle and snuff it with your fingers and throw away the burning bit of wick among the shavings.

Manders.   Did you see that?

Engstrand.   Yes, distinctly.

Manders.   I can't understand it at all. It is never my habit to snuff a candle with my fingers.

Engstrand.   Yes, it wasn't like you to do that, sir. But who would have thought it could be such a dangerous thing to do?

Manders (walking restlessly backwards and forwards).   Oh, don't ask me!

Engstrand (following him about).   And you hadn't insured it either, had you, sir?

Manders.   No, no, no; you heard me say so.

Engstrand.   You hadn't insured it—and then went and set light to the whole place! Good Lord, what bad luck!

Manders (wiping the perspiration from his forehead).   You may well say so, Engstrand.

Engstrand.   And that it should happen to a charitable institution that would have been of service both to the town and the country, so to speak! The newspapers won't be very kind to your reverence, I expect.

Manders.   No, that is just what I am thinking of. It is almost the worst part of the whole thing. The spiteful attacks and accusations—it is horrible to think of!

Mrs. Alving (coming in from the garden).   I can't get him away from the fire.

Manders.   Oh, there you are, Mrs. Alving.

Mrs. Alving.   You will escape having to make your inaugural address now, at all events, Mr. Manders.

Manders.   Oh, I would so gladly have———

Mrs. Alving (in a dull voice).   It is just as well it has happened. This Orphanage would never have come to any good.

Manders.   Don't you think so?

Mrs. Alving.   Do you?

Manders.   But it is none the less an extraordinary piece of ill luck.

Mrs. Alving.   We will discuss it simply as a business matter.—Are you waiting for Mr. Manders, Engstrand?

Engstrand (at the hall door).   Yes, I am.

Mrs. Alving.   Sit down then, while you are waiting.

Engstrand.   Thank you, I would rather stand.

Mrs. Alving (to MANDERS*).*   I suppose you are going by the boat?

Manders.   Yes. It goes in about an hour.

Mrs. Alving.   Please take all the documents back with you. I don't want to hear another word about the matter. I have something else to think about now——

Manders.   Mrs. Alving——

Mrs. Alving.   Later on I will send you a power of attorney to deal with it exactly as you please.

Manders.   I shall be most happy to undertake that. I am afraid the original intention of the bequest will have to be entirely altered now.

Mrs. Alving.   Of course.

Manders.   Provisionally, I should suggest this way of disposing of it. Make over the Solvik property to the parish. The land is undoubtedly not without a certain value; it will always be useful for some purpose or another. And as for the interest on the remaining capital that is on deposit in the bank, possibly I might make suitable use of that in support of some undertaking that promises to be of use to the town.

Mrs. Alving.   Do exactly as you please. The whole thing is a matter of indifference to me now.

Engstrand.   You will think of my Sailors' Home, Mr. Manders?

Manders.   Yes, certainly, that is a suggestion. But we must consider the matter carefully.

Engstrand (aside).   Consider!—devil take it! Oh Lord.

Manders (sighing).   And unfortunately I can't tell how much longer I may have anything to do with the matter—whether public opinion may not force me to retire from it altogether. That depends entirely upon the result of the enquiry into the cause of the fire.

Mrs. Alving.   What do you say?

Manders.   And one cannot in any way reckon upon the result beforehand.

Engstrand (going nearer to him).   Yes, indeed one can; because here stand I, Jacob Engstrand.

Manders. Quite so, but————

Engstrand (lowering his voice). And Jacob Engstrand isn't the man to desert a worthy benefactor in the hour of need, as the saying is.

Manders. Yes, but, my dear fellow—how————?

Engstrand. You might say Jacob Engstrand is an angel of salvation, so to speak, your reverence.

Manders. No, no, I couldn't possibly accept that.

Engstrand. That's how it will be, all the same. I know someone who has taken the blame for someone else on his shoulders before now, I do.

Manders. Jacob! *(Grasps his hand.)* You are one in a thousand! You shall have assistance in the matter of your Sailors' Home, you may rely upon that.

[ENGSTRAND *tries to thank him, but is prevented by emotion.*]

Manders (hanging his wallet over his shoulder). Now we must be off. We will travel together.

Engstrand (by the dining-room door, says aside to REGINA:*)* Come with me, you hussy! You shall be as cosy as the yolk in an egg!

Regina (tossing her head). Merci!

[*She goes out into the hall and brings back* MANDER'S *luggage.*]

Manders. Good-bye, Mrs. Alving! And may the spirit of order and of what is lawful speedily enter into this house.

Mrs. Alving. Good-bye, Mr. Manders.

[*She goes into the conservatory, as she sees* OSWALD *coming in by the garden door.*]

Engstrand (as he and REGINA *are helping* MANDERS *on with his coat).* Good-bye, my child. And if anything should happen to you, you know where Jacob Engstrand is to be found. *(Lowering his voice.)* Little Harbour Street, ahem————! *(To* MRS. ALVING *and* OSWALD.*)* And my house for poor seafaring men shall be called the "Alving Home," it shall. And, if I can carry out my own ideas about it, I shall make bold to hope that it may be worthy of bearing the late Mr. Alving's name.

Manders (at the door). Ahem—ahem! Come along, my dear Engstrand. Good-bye—good-bye!

[*He and* ENGSTRAND *go out by the hall door.*]

Oswald (going to the table). What house was he speaking about?

Mrs. Alving. I believe it is some sort of a Home that he and Mr. Manders want to start.

Oswald. It will be burnt up just like this one.

Mrs. Alving. What makes you think that?

Oswald. Everything will be burnt up; nothing will be left that is in memory of my father. Here am I being burnt up, too.

[REGINA *looks at him in alarm.*]

Mrs. Alving. Oswald! You should not have stayed so long over there, my poor boy.

Oswald (sitting down at the table). I almost believe you are right.

Mrs. Alving. Let me dry your face, Oswald; you are all wet.

[*Wipes his face with her handkerchief.*]

Oswald (looking straight before him, with no expression in his eyes). Thank you, mother.

Mrs. Alving. And aren't you tired, Oswald? Don't you want to go to sleep?

Oswald (uneasily). No, no—not to sleep! I never sleep; I only pretend to. (*Gloomily.*) That will come soon enough.

Mrs. Alving (looking at him anxiously). Anyhow you are really ill, my darling boy.

Regina (intently). Is Mr. Alving ill?

Oswald (impatiently). And do shut all the doors! This deadly fear——

Mrs. Alving. Shut the doors, Regina. (REGINA *shuts the doors and remains standing by the hall door.* MRS. ALVING *takes off her shawl;* REGINA *does the same.* MRS. ALVING *draws up a chair near to* OSWALD'S *and sits down beside him.*) That's it! Now I will sit beside you——

Oswald. Yes, do. And Regina must stay in here too. Regina must always be near me. You must give me a helping hand, you know, Regina. Won't you do that?

Regina. I don't understand——

Mrs. Alving. A helping hand?

Oswald. Yes—when there is need for it.

Mrs. Alving. Oswald, have you not your mother to give you a helping hand?

Oswald. You? (*Smiles.*) No, mother, you will never give me the kind of helping hand I mean. (*Laughs grimly.*) You? Ha, ha! (*Looks gravely at her.*) After all, you have the best right. (*Impetuously.*) Why don't you call me by my Christian name, Regina? Why don't you say Oswald?

Regina (in a low voice). I did not think Mrs. Alving would like it.

Mrs. Alving. It will not be long before you have the right to do it. Sit down here now beside us, too. (REGINA *sits down quietly and hesitatingly at the other side of the table.*) And now, my poor tortured boy, I am going to take the burden off your mind——

Oswald.   You, mother?

Mrs. Alving.   ———all that you call remorse and regret and self-reproach.

Oswald.   And you think you can do that?

Mrs. Alving.   Yes, now I can, Oswald. A little while ago you were talking about the joy of life, and what you said seemed to shed a new light upon everything in my whole life.

Oswald (shaking his head).   I don't in the least understand what you mean.

Mrs. Alving.   You should have known your father in his young days in the army. He was full of the joy of life, I can tell you.

Oswald.   Yes, I know.

Mrs. Alving.   It gave me a holiday feeling only to look at him, full of irrepressible energy and exuberant spirits.

Oswald.   What then?

Mrs. Alving.   Well, then this boy, full of the joy of life—for he was just like a boy, then—had to make his home in a second-rate town which had none of the joy of life to offer him, but only dissipations. He had to come out here and live an aimless life; he had only an official post. He had no work worth devoting his whole mind to; he had nothing more than official routine to attend to. He had not a single companion capable of appreciating what the joy of life meant; nothing but idlers and tipplers———

Oswald.   Mother———!

Mrs. Alving.   And so the inevitable happened!

Oswald.   What was the inevitable?

Mrs. Alving.   You said yourself this evening what would happen in your case if you stayed at home.

Oswald.   Do you mean by that, that father———?

Mrs. Alving.   Your poor father never found any outlet for the overmastering joy of life that was in him. And I brought no holiday spirit into his home, either.

Oswald.   You didn't, either?

Mrs. Alving.   I had been taught about duty, and the sort of thing that I believed in so long here. Everything seemed to turn upon duty—my duty, or his duty—and I am afraid I made your poor father's home unbearable to him, Oswald.

Oswald.   Why did you never say anything about it to me in your letters?

Mrs. Alving.   I never looked at it as a thing I could speak of to you, who were his son.

Oswald.   What way did you look at it, then?

Mrs. Alving.   I only saw the one fact, that your father was a lost man before ever you were born.

Oswald (in a choking voice).   Ah————!

[*He gets up and goes to the window.*]

Mrs. Alving.   And then I had the one thought in my mind, day and night, that Regina in fact had as good a right in this house—as my own boy had.

Oswald (turns round suddenly).   Regina————?

Regina (gets up and asks in choking tones).   I————?

Mrs. Alving.   Yes, now you both know it.

Oswald.   Regina!

Regina (to herself).   So mother was one of that sort too.

Mrs. Alving.   Your mother had many good qualities, Regina.

Regina.   Yes, but she was one of that sort too, all the same. I have even thought so myself, sometimes, but————. Then, if you please, Mrs. Alving, may I have permission to leave at once?

Mrs. Alving.   Do you really wish to, Regina?

Regina.   Yes, indeed, I certainly wish to.

Mrs. Alving.   Of course you shall do as you like, but————

Oswald (going to REGINA*).*   Leave now? This is your home.

Regina.   *Merci*, Mr. Alving—oh, of course I may say Oswald now, but that is not the way I thought it would become allowable.

Mrs. Alving.   Regina, I have not been open with you————

Regina.   No, I can't say you have! If I had known Oswald was ill————. And now that there can never be anything serious between us————. No, I really can't stay here in the country and wear myself out looking after invalids.

Oswald.   Not even for the sake of one who has so near a claim on you?

Regina.   No, indeed I can't. A poor girl must make some use of her youth, otherwise she may easily find herself out in the cold before she knows where she is. And I have got the joy of life in me, too, Mrs. Alving.

Mrs. Alving.   Yes, unfortunately; but don't throw yourself away, Regina.

Regina.   Oh, what's going to happen will happen. If Oswald takes after his father, it is just as likely I take after my mother, I expect.———— May I ask, Mrs. Alving, whether Mr. Manders knows this about me?

Mrs. Alving.   Mr. Manders knows everything.

Regina (putting on her shawl).   Oh, well then, the best thing I can do is to get away by the boat as soon as I can. Mr. Manders is such a nice gentleman to deal with; and it certainly seems to me that I have just as much right to some of that money as he—as that horrid carpenter.

Mrs. Alving.   You are quite welcome to it, Regina.

Regina (looking at her fixedly).   You might as well have brought me up like a gentleman's daughter; it would have been more suitable. *(Tosses her head.)* Oh, well—never mind! *(With a bitter glance at the unopened bottle.)* I daresay some day I shall be drinking champagne with gentlefolk, after all.

Mrs. Alving.   If ever you need a home, Regina, come to me.

Regina.   No, thank you, Mrs. Alving. Mr. Manders takes an interest in me, I know. And if things should go very badly with me, I know one house at any rate where I shall feel at home.

Mrs. Alving.   Where is that?

Regina.   In the "Alving Home."

Mrs. Alving.   Regina—I can see quite well—you are going to your ruin!

Regina.   Pooh!—good-bye.

[*She bows to them and goes out through the hall.*]

Oswald (standing by the window and looking out).   Has she gone?

Mrs. Alving.   Yes.

Oswald (muttering to himself).   I think it's all wrong.

Mrs. Alving (going up to him from behind and putting her hands on his shoulders).   Oswald, my dear boy—has it been a great shock to you?

Oswald (turning his face towards her).   All this about father, do you mean?

Mrs. Alving.   Yes, about your unhappy father. I am so afraid it may have been too much for you.

Oswald.   What makes you think that? Naturally it has taken me entirely by surprise; but, after all, I don't know that it matters much to me.

Mrs. Alving (drawing back her hands).   Doesn't matter!—that your father's life was such a terrible failure!

Oswald.   Of course I can feel sympathy for him, just as I would for anyone else, but——

Mrs. Alving.   No more than that! For your own father!

Oswald (impatiently).   Father—father! I never knew anything of my father. I don't remember anything else about him except that he once made me sick.

Mrs. Alving. It is dreadful to think of!—But surely a child should feel some affection for his father, whatever happens?

Oswald. When the child has nothing to thank his father for? When he has never known him? Do you really cling to that antiquated superstition—you, who are so broad-minded in other things?

Mrs. Alving. You call it nothing but a superstition!

Oswald. Yes, and you can see that for yourself quite well, mother. It is one of those beliefs that are put into circulation in the world, and———

Mrs. Alving. Ghosts of beliefs!

Oswald (walking across the room). Yes, you might call them ghosts.

Mrs. Alving (with an outburst of feeling). Oswald—then you don't love me either.

Oswald. You I know, at any rate———

Mrs. Alving. You know me, yes; but is that all?

Oswald. And I know how fond you are of me, and I ought to be grateful to you for that. Besides, you can be so tremendously useful to me, now that I am ill.

Mrs. Alving. Yes, can't I, Oswald! I could almost bless your illness, as it has driven you home to me. For I see quite well that you are not my very own yet; you must be won.

Oswald (impatiently). Yes, yes, yes; all that is just a way of talking. You must remember I am a sick man, mother. I can't concern myself much with anyone else; I have enough to do, thinking about myself.

Mrs. Alving (gently). I will be very good and patient.

Oswald. And cheerful too, mother!

Mrs. Alving. Yes, my dear boy, you are quite right. *(Goes up to him.)* Now have I taken away all your remorse and self-reproach?

Oswald. Yes, you have done that. But who will take away the fear?

Mrs. Alving. The fear?

Oswald (crossing the room). Regina would have done it for one kind word.

Mrs. Alving. I don't understand you. What fear do you mean—and what has Regina to do with it?

Oswald. Is it very late, mother?

Mrs. Alving. It is early morning. *(Looks out through the conservatory windows.)* The dawn is breaking already on the heights. And the sky is clear, Oswald. In a little while you will see the sun.

Oswald. I am glad of that. After all, there may be many things yet for me to be glad of and to live for———

Mrs. Alving.   I should hope so!

Oswald.   Even if I am not able to work———

Mrs. Alving.   You will soon find you are able to work again now, my dear boy. You have no longer all those painful depressing thoughts to brood over.

Oswald.   No, it is a good thing that you have been able to rid me of those fancies. If only, now, I could overcome this one thing———. *(Sits down on the couch.)* Let us have a little chat, mother.

Mrs. Alving.   Yes, let us.

[*Pushes an armchair near to the couch and sits down beside him.*]

Oswald.   The sun is rising—and you know all about it; so I don't feel the fear any longer.

Mrs. Alving.   I know all about what?

Oswald (without listening to her).   Mother, isn't it the case that you said this evening there was nothing in the world you would not do for me if I asked you?

Mrs. Alving.   Yes, certainly I said so.

Oswald.   And will you be as good as your word, mother?

Mrs. Alving.   You may rely upon that, my own dear boy. I have nothing else to live for, but you.

Oswald.   Yes, yes; well, listen to me, mother. You are very strong-minded, I know. I want you to sit quite quiet when you hear what I am going to tell you.

Mrs. Alving.   But what is this dreadful thing———?

Oswald.   You mustn't scream. Do you hear? Will you promise me that? We are going to sit and talk it over quite quietly. Will you promise me that, mother?

Mrs. Alving.   Yes, yes, I promise—only tell me what it is.

Oswald.   Well, then, you must know that this fatigue of mine—and my not being able to think about my work—all that is not really the illness itself———

Mrs. Alving.   What is the illness itself?

Oswald.   What I am suffering from is hereditary; it—*(touches his forehead, and speaks very quietly)*—it lies here.

Mrs. Alving (almost speechless).   Oswald! No—no!

Oswald.   Don't scream; I can't stand it. Yes, I tell you, it lies here, waiting. And any time, any moment, it may break out.

Mrs. Alving.   How horrible———!

Oswald.   Do keep quiet. That is the state I am in———

Mrs. Alving (springing up). It isn't true, Oswald! It is impossible! It can't be that!

Oswald. I had one attack while I was abroad. It passed off quickly. But when I learnt the condition I had been in, then this dreadful haunting fear took possession of me.

Mrs. Alving. That was the fear, then ————

Oswald. Yes, it is so indescribably horrible, you know. If only it had been an ordinary mortal disease ————. I am not so much afraid of dying; though, of course, I should like to live as long as I can.

Mrs. Alving. Yes, yes, Oswald, you must!

Oswald. But this is so appallingly horrible. To become like a helpless child again—to have to be fed, to have to be ————. Oh, it's unspeakable!

Mrs. Alving. My child has his mother to tend him.

Oswald (jumping up). No, never; that is just what I won't endure! I dare not think what it would mean to linger on like that for years—to get old and grey like that. And you might die before I did. *(Sits down in* MRS. ALVING'S *chair.)* Because it doesn't necessarily have a fatal end quickly, the doctor said. He called it a kind of softening of the brain— or something of that sort. *(Smiles mournfully.)* I think that expression sounds so nice. It always makes me think of cherry-coloured velvet curtains—something that is soft to stroke.

Mrs. Alving (with a scream). Oswald!

Oswald (jumps up and walks about the room). And now you have taken Regina from me! If I had only had her. She would have given me a helping hand, I know.

Mrs. Alving (going up to him). What do you mean, my darling boy? Is there any help in the world I would not be willing to give you?

Oswald. When I had recovered from the attack I had abroad, the doctor told me that when it recurred—and it will recur—there would be no more hope.

Mrs. Alving. And he was heartless enough to ————

Oswald. I insisted on knowing. I told him I had arrangements to make ————. *(Smiles cunningly.)* And so I had. *(Takes a small box from his inner breast-pocket.)* Mother, do you see this?

Mrs. Alving. What is it?

Oswald. Morphia powders.

Mrs. Alving (looking at him in terror). Oswald—my boy!

Oswald. I have twelve of them saved up ————

Mrs. Alving (snatching at it). Give me the box, Oswald!

Oswald. Not yet, mother.

[*Puts it back in his pocket.*]

Mrs. Alving. I shall never get over this!

Oswald. You must. If I had had Regina here now, I would have told her quietly how things stand with me—and asked her to give me this last helping hand. She would have helped me, I am certain.

Mrs. Alving. Never!

Oswald. If this horrible thing had come upon me and she had seen me lying helpless, like a baby, past help, past saving, past hope—with no chance of recovering————

Mrs. Alving. Never in the world would Regina have done it.

Oswald. Regina would have done it. Regina was so splendidly light-hearted. And she would very soon have tired of looking after an invalid like me.

Mrs. Alving. Then thank heaven Regina is not here!

Oswald. Well, now you have got to give me that helping hand, mother.

Mrs. Alving (with a loud scream). I!

Oswald. Who has a better right than you?

Mrs. Alving. I? Your mother!

Oswald. Just for that reason.

Mrs. Alving. I, who gave you your life!

Oswald. I never asked you for life. And what kind of a life was it that you gave me? I don't want it! You shall take it back!

Mrs. Alving. Help! Help!

[*Runs into the hall.*]

Oswald (following her). Don't leave me! Where are you going?

Mrs. Alving (in the hall). To fetch the doctor to you, Oswald! Let me out!

Oswald (going into the hall). You shan't go out. And no one shall come in.

[*Turns the key in the lock.*]

Mrs. Alving (coming in again). Oswald! Oswald!—my child!

Oswald (following her). Have you a mother's heart—and can bear to see me suffering this unspeakable terror?

Mrs. Alving (controlling herself, after a moment's silence). There is my hand on it.

Oswald. Will you————?

Mrs. Alving. If it becomes necessary. But it shan't become necessary. No, no—it is impossible it should!

Oswald. Let us hope so. And let us live together as long as we can. Thank you, mother.

> [*He sits down in the armchair, which* MRS. ALVING *had moved beside the couch. Day is breaking; the lamp is still burning on the table.*]

Mrs. Alving (coming cautiously nearer). Do you feel calmer now?

Oswald. Yes.

Mrs. Alving (bending over him). It has only been a dreadful fancy of yours, Oswald! Nothing but fancy. All this upset has been bad for you. But now you will get some rest, at home with your own mother, my darling boy. You shall have everything you want, just as you did when you were a little child.—There, now. The attack is over. You see how easily it passed off! I knew it would.—And look, Oswald, what a lovely day we are going to have? Brilliant sunshine. Now you will be able to see your home properly.

> [*She goes to the table and puts out the lamp. It is sunrise. The glaciers and peaks in the distance are seen bathed in bright morning light.*]

Oswald (who has been sitting motionless in the armchair, with his back to the scene outside, suddenly says:) Mother, give me the sun.

Mrs. Alving (standing at the table, and looking at him in amazement). What do you say?

Oswald (repeats in a dull, toneless voice). The sun—the sun.

Mrs. Alving (going up to him). Oswald, what is the matter with you? (OSWALD *seems to shrink up in the chair; all his muscles relax; his face loses its expression, and his eyes stare stupidly.* MRS. ALVING *is trembling with terror.*) What is it! (*Screams.*) Oswald! What is the matter with you! (*Throws herself on her knees beside him and shakes him.*) Oswald! Oswald! Look at me! Don't you know me!

Oswald (in an expressionless voice, as before). The sun—the sun.

Mrs. Alving (jumps up despairingly, beats her head with her hands, and screams). I can't bear it! (*Whispers as though paralysed with fear.*) I can't bear it! Never! (*Suddenly.*) Where has he got it? (*Passes her hand quickly over his coat.*) Here! (*Draws back a little way and cries:*) No, no, no!—Yes!—no, no!

> [*She stands a few steps from him, her hands thrust into her hair, and stares at him in speechless terror.*]

Oswald (sitting motionless, as before). The sun—the sun.